EARL OF WAINTHORPE

For the Love of an Earl, Book One

COLLETTE CAMERON

Blue Rose Romance®

Sweet-to-Spicy Timeless Romance®

EARL OF WAINTHORPE
For the Love of an Earl
Copyright © 2023 Collette Cameron®
Cover Art: Angela Horner-Long Valley Designs

Attn: Permissions Coordinator
Blue Rose Romance®
P.O. Box 167, Scappoose, OR 97056

ISBN Paperback: 9781954307674
ISBN eBook: 9781954307667
www.collettecameron.com

"In fact, I'll up the stakes, my sweet.

You'll plead for much more than my kisses."

Other Collette Cameron Books

For the Love of an Earl
Earl of Wainthorpe
Earl of Scarborough
Earl of Keyworth
Earl of Renshaw

Check out Collette's Other Series
Castle Brides
Heart of a Scot
Seductive Scoundrels
The Culpepper Misses
The Honorable Rogues®
Chronicles of the Westbrook Brides
Highland Heather Romancing a Scot
Daughters of Desire (Scandalous Ladies)

Dedication

While I was writing the final chapters of EARL OF WAINTHORPE, my mother's health took a turn for the worse, and she entered Hospice care. The compassionate physicians, nurses, certified nurse assistants, social workers—even the hospital cleaning staff—who tended her brought me great peace of mind. My mother passed away while I was editing EARL OF WAINTHORPE.

I dedicate this, my twenty-first book to often overworked and under-appreciated healthcare workers. Thank you for your dedication, commitment, sacrifice, and sympathy.

1

18 May 1817

London, England

By thunder. At long last, Pierce had the poltroon. Idly grazing his thumb along the lower edges of his playing cards, he raised his gaze to meet Bertram Normand's, the twelfth Baron Fairfax, triumphant stare. Mindful to keep his expression bored, Pierce brushed an indifferent glance over the former soldier. His regard lingered for a fraction on the crescent-shaped scar marring Fairfax's right hand before he directed his attention once more to his opponent's flushed face.

"Well, Wainthorpe?" Fairfax wheezed. "Ready to

concede defeat?"

The other players, James, the amiable Earl of Pembroke, and Alistair, Earl of Benton, exchanged a swift glance. Did they sense this was more than a simple game of Loo?

The perspiration beading the baron's forehead, as well as the repeated darting of his tongue to moisten the corners of his mouth, exposed the older man's excitement. From the cunning glint in his bloodshot blue eyes, he thought sure he had won this hand.

Newly titled, in debt up to his sly brows, his estates mortgaged to their regal cornices and corbels, and possessed of an insatiable thirst for spirits, Fairfax needed to win—was bloody desperate to, actually.

Pierce, on the other hand, was not.

Already an earl and the successor to a duchy, he had also inherited a substantial sum from his East Indian Munda mother. Which not only made him rich but, more importantly, powerful. And hell-bent on retribution because of the actions of the man sitting opposite him.

Three pairs of gazes—two congenial, if somewhat glassy from indulging in the expensive cognac Lady

Lockhart provided—peered at Pierce expectantly across the table. Teeming with cocky self-confidence, Fairfax believed he had Pierce by the ballocks.

Exactly what Pierce had manipulated him into thinking.

So easy to do, too.

A frustrated frown here. A hefty sigh there. Nervously playing his fingertips atop the table. Even an occasional grimace or biting the corner of his mouth.

Each a calculated sham. All with one purpose.

To lure Fairfax into a snare he couldn't escape from.

Pierce's blood hummed through his veins in anticipation, a satisfying mantra of long-awaited vindication. He expected to feel more elation, more exhilaration. After all, he'd waited two decades for this moment.

True, for a man accustomed to doing what he wanted, who enjoyed thumbing his nose at the *haut ton's* strictures, and whose position and influence made most things possible with an idle flick of his finger, excitement was a rare commodity.

That must be it.

He had been bored, restless, discontent for so long that nothing much stirred him anymore. He needed a challenge. Something invigorating. Outrageous. Scandalous even. Anything to shake him from this unfeeling stupor.

An urgent whisper, the voice melodic yet heavy with censure and distress, interrupted the tense silence. A tall, lithe woman had maneuvered her way to stand beside the baron. "Halt this idiocy at once. I insist you come away now—"

Awareness prickled across Pierce's shoulders and down his backbone.

Who the devil was she?

"Cease your endless harping, gel," Fairfax snapped, his florid face flaming darker. His vehement head shake sent his mutton-chop adorned jowls to jiggling. Harrumphing his annoyance again, he yanked on his ear while cutting her a rancorous look. "Or I shall send you packing back to Elmswood Parke tonight?"

"Horse feathers and hen's teeth, Cousin." Her cute

nose scrunching the tiniest bit, she shook her fan at him much the same as a cat twitches its tail when piqued. "We both know you'll do no such thing."

An overtone of proud defiance tempered her response.

Cutting his hand toward her, Fairfax grumbled into his brandy glass. "Don' know why I let you talk me into draggin' you to London."

"Because, *Cousin,* doors are open to me that you cannot place your shoes-in-desperate- need-of-a-good- polish anywhere near."

She sounded more matter-of-fact than boastful or sarcastic, and Pierce found himself rather admiring her pluck.

"You're jus' an extra 'spense I can ill afford." The baron eyed the cache atop the table, a distinct lustful glint crinkling the corners of his eyes. Obviously peeved, he scratched his jaw. "And with a tongue sharp enough to curl the bark off a Scotch pine, a constant, aggravating pain in my arse."

Slapping his knee, he dissolved into a fit of short-lived laughter.

"That would be your gout paining you from too much meat and drink." Twin spots of color accenting her high cheekbones, she squared her shoulders, slanted her chin to a regal angle, and with an agile twist of her long fingers, unfurled her fan. "And I might add, your eloquent speech continues to stagger."

Fairfax's ready glower checked the titters and chuckles accompanying her retort, but not Pierce's reluctant smile.

By Jove, she was bloody entertaining.

Another time, Pierce might've appreciated the woman's barbed rejoinders much more. Instead, he only spared her a cursory glance.

Nonetheless, he quite liked what he saw.

Pierce appreciated willowy, feminine forms. From beneath his hooded gaze, he cut her another covert glance. Not a woman that was easily forgotten or disregarded.

She noticed his perusal and arched a winged eyebrow. The tiniest hint of chagrin shadowed the edges of her oval face.

Pierce forced his focus back to the game.

He'd anticipated this opportunity, planned and schemed for this moment for far too many years to entertain pity for Fairfax's treatment of the chit. Besides, except for his sisters and nieces, Pierce never—*truly never*—harbored any sentiment stronger than warm regard toward females.

The rustle of fine silks and satins and the rhythmic swishing of ladies' fans increased. More privileged and jaded guests took note of the high stakes and maneuvered nearer the table to witness the outcome. Their anticipation tangible, they approached, much like hounds closing in on a prey's fresh scent.

"We are waiting, Wainthorpe. Are you in or out?"

Fairfax played his fingers along the table's edge. Then, as if realizing his actions exposed his uneasiness, he bent his other hand and casually touched two knuckles to his mouth.

Patience was not the baron's strong suit, and Pierce intended to use that flaw against him.

"Let's dispense with tokens, shall we?" An eyebrow and his mouth quirked, Pierce shoved the entire stack of notes before him to the table's center.

Fans swished faster as muffled gasps and one low whistle accompanied his brazen move. Many peers' fortunes had been reversed with the careless flip of a card or a toss of dice. Doubtless the onlookers thought him a hapless fool or an idiot who'd taken leave of his senses.

Those were two of the more polite things London's upper crust called him.

Their opinions meant naught, however.

Never had. Never would.

Years ago, when he'd first arrived in England, these same people had elevated their noses or pulled their skirts aside when he came near. His half-Munda heritage was a black mark upon him. As if ancestry and lineage molded a person's character for good or bad. Many of the blue-bloods standing nearby kept secrets well-hidden that were far more objectionable than his mixed blood.

So at every opportunity, Pierce tossed their conventions and rules to the wind. More like kicked them to next winter. Only of late, even that ceased producing the usual wry twist of his lips.

Tonight, however, he was intent on one thing.

Pierce trained his full attention on the man across the table from him.

A man he despised with every deceptively calm breath he drew. Since, as a small, terrified lad of seven, he bit the then Captain Normand's hand until the coppery taste of blood had filled Pierce's mouth. Before the cull cudgeled him with the butt of his pistol.

Hours later, he'd awoken, blood blurring his vision, and saw his *AamA*, his mother…

Not now!

Pierce bore a scar an inch above his right temple from that blow. A reminder of why he despised Fairfax each time he glanced into a mirror or touched the triangular mark. Jaw clamped until his teeth threatened to crack, Pierce dropped his gaze to the ante. A quick calculation sent his pulse stampeding.

Just under five and seventy thousand pounds.

Since Fairfax had inherited the barony and skulked back to England a year ago, Pierce had systematically bought the baron's debts. Those, along with tonight's losses, would pitch the unconscionable devil's spawn, bulbous nose over fat arse, into bankruptcy.

Destitution. Ruination.

No. This was justice; blast Fairfax's black soul to perdition.

Pierce's pulse surged, and his stomach clenched into a gnarled tangle of anticipation, revenge, satisfaction, and *yes*—a trifling stab of remembered pain. Yet, as was his habit, he arranged his features into passiveness. Something he mastered as a child to buffer the scorn and ridicule often directed toward him by the upper ten thousand.

So close now, AamA.

Would Fairfax take the bait?

Would his greed and arrogance plummet him into the gutters where he belonged?

"I'm no fool." Chuckling and shaking his head,

Pembroke laid his cards neatly upon the table, then pushed them away. Relaxing into his chair, he tossed back the last of his cognac while eyeing Pierce and their cohort, Benton, over the glass's rim.

A small pin—the letter W—on their tailored jacket lapels revealed their membership in the exclusive Wicked Earls' Club. A secret society for unrepentant and wholly irredeemable rakes and rapscallions. No one but the members knew the pins' significance. If an earl lost all sense of reason and took that fateful step into matrimony, he must still protect the identity of the remaining unshackled peers.

"Aye, neither am I." Benton too, surrendered his cards. Though the Scot simply tossed his hand, face upward, onto the rosewood card table. He lifted his glass toward Pierce, mischief cavorting in his acute blue eyes. "Who would you lay odds on, Pembroke?" he asked in the King's clipped English, only the subtlest hint of a brogue flavoring his precise speech.

A grin tugged Pembroke's mouth upward, and he scratched his eyebrow. "Well, truth be told, Loo has never really been Wainthorpe's game. Too civilized."

"True, he's more of a hazard or racing sort." Benton gave Pierce a measured nod and picked a piece of lint from his cuff. He sliced Pierce a considering glance. "So hard to read that emotionless expression. Sometimes his eyes reveal a wee bit of something if you look carefully."

"Always been like that." Pembroke grasped the etched decanter and raised it, silently asking who wanted another tot. Receiving affirmative nods, he poured a finger's worth for everyone.

Fairfax immediately quaffed a mouthful.

"Remember at Eton when he broke his arm?" Pembroke jerked his chin toward Pierce. "No tears or caterwauling. Just blinked those obsidian eyes."

"If you're going to discuss me, can you at least do it when I'm not present?" For decades those two had tried their utmost to get a reaction from Pierce. All in good-natured ribbing that close chums who'd experienced hard times together are permitted.

The baron stared at Pierce, his lined face crumpling

in puzzlement. He narrowed his eyes to discerning slits.

"Are you positive we haven't played together before, Wainthorpe?" Fairfax asked. "I cannot help but think we have met prior to this. You seem slightly familiar."

He still did not recognize Pierce. But why should he?

The last time Fairfax saw him, Pierce had been a scrawny, shaggy-haired lad.

"I'm certain I have never sat at a card table with you, Fairfax." Truth there. "Are you in or not?"

Pierce knew full well the sot didn't possess a shilling more. He made a point to learn all he could about Fairfax. Probably knew more about his finances and state of affairs than the man himself.

His pretty relative, though?

Well, she had been unexpected. And Pierce loathed being on the receiving end of surprises.

His man would be explaining that glaring—*lovely*—oversight on the morrow.

Pierce had no interest in the baron's estates nor in

his few heads of livestock. Nonetheless, he intended to leave the man with nothing. Not even a pot to piss in, as Pierce's former sailor-turned-manservant, Popplewell, was wont to quote.

Failure to honor his gambling debts meant complete disgrace for Fairfax. At present, he hovered on Polite Society's outermost fringes. A scandal would tip him over that fragile edge into ignominy. He would be blacklisted from *le beau monde's* elite assemblies he so admired, unable to purchase something as economical as a piece of straw on credit.

Not a qualm or jot of hesitation muddled Pierce's resolve.

The baron deserved every misfortune directed his way.

What about his cousin, Pritam, my son? She's done you no harm.

Pierce could almost hear his gentle mother's musical voice chastising him for his cruelty.

It mattered not. He craved justice.

For her.

For the small child who held his dying mother in his skinny arms, begging her not to leave him. For his father, who perished of fever scarcely two short months later, brought on by a broken heart. For his three older half-sisters, also left parentless, though they were well into their late teens and early twenties when Father passed.

Spearing the woman a glance, Pierce's gaze tangled with hers, entreaty fairly radiating from her unusual umber-colored eyes. Eyes a shade lighter than the abundant auburn lashes framing them and the shiny tresses pulled back from her forehead and pinned into a rather severe knot for someone so young. Not a traditional beauty; nonetheless, her features were striking, fine-boned, and compelled him to indulge in a lingering look.

Which caused the queerest surge behind his ribs.

It was her almond-shaped, cinnamon eyes.

Steady and assessing, filled with lively intelligence and a hint of something almost exotic. Wild. Untamed even.

Her gown, however, did nothing for her creamy complexion. A revolting hue somewhere between a Pompeian deep red and spoiled salmon, the frock was an ill-fitting travesty of questionable origin. That seamstress ought not to touch a needle again. Ever.

Something very near compassion dared to try to well within his breast. He broke eye contact and soundly mashed the emotion flat as a newssheet whilst laying his cards face down atop the table.

She was Fairfax's kin.

He'd brought this undoing upon her, not Pierce.

"Am I to assume your hesitation means no, Fairfax?" Pierce angled to sweep the winnings to his side of the small table.

"Hold there. No need for haste." Fairfax made a curt gesture, a flicker of unease drawing his beetle brows tight. His stubby tongue appeared at the corner of his mouth once again, and he tore his lustful gaze from the ante. "You'll accept my marker, of course?"

The poorest church's alms box held more coins than the baron's shallow pockets.

"Guaranteeing what, precisely? 'Tis well known, you're already in dun territory." Idly fingering a token, Pierce's blasted attention gravitated to the coppery-headed cousin once more.

Her gaze inquisitive, she angled her head, the slightest crease pulling her inner eyebrows together over her little button of a nose.

Devil take it.

Slight slip there, mentioning Fairfax's financial status, and she honed in on it with swift shrewdness. It wouldn't do to reveal too much. The baron might get suspicious, which could lead to a case of nerves and his withdrawal from the game.

The moment passed, and Fairfax didn't seem to notice, although a troubled frown still lined his cousin's pretty face.

"Your vowels aren't worth the foolscap you've written them on, Fairfax." Triumph tunneled through Pierce's blood as the baron's countenance flushed claret red, the veins standing out on his nose and forehead, a convoluted map of despair.

The cousin's expression remained a bland alabaster mask, but she couldn't silence her gaze. With each slow sweep of her lashes, she denounced Pierce and Fairfax. Something else gleamed in those captivating eyes, too.

Pierce shook his head, his smile tight and taunting. "No, I'm afraid I must insist on something more substantial. Something tangible. Something I can lay my hands on other than a slip of useless paper."

Fairfax puffed out his cheeks and exhaled. "Fine. Fine then." With a jerk of his sausage-like finger, he signaled a footman for foolscap and ink. "I shall make a sport of Elmswood Parke. It's not entailed."

Another gasp, this one distraught and feminine, rent the air. The cousin, her hands clasped before her, her face ashen, shook her head. An unexpectedly wild, nutmeg-hued strand sprang loose of its tight confines and teased the delicate hollow where her ear and neck joined.

Unanticipated desire sluiced through Pierce, and he was flabbergasted to realize he envied the jaunty curl. He longed to place his lips atop the sensitive spot and see if her skin was as satiny as it appeared. To discover what intriguing scent she wore, if any.

Those unwarranted ponderings earned her a speculative look.

Innocents did not typically appeal to him. Redheads didn't usually either.

"Bertram. Please, you cannot stake my—our home," she implored, touching his shoulder and revealing the neatly mended tips of her worn gloves. "If you should lose…"

She had experienced want and deprivation. Pierce would bet his prized, matched bays on it. Yet she fairly glowed with poise, not a hint of inferiority bowing her head or shoulders as she implored the baron.

Pierce felt acute mortification on her behalf. A first for him, and by thunder, he didn't like it by half.

With a half-oath, half-growl, Fairfax rounded on her, his protruding belly jostling the table. "I can, and I shall. Know your place, Bianca Salisbury."

"I assure you, I am *well* aware of my station." Her fisted clasp upon her fan suggested she fought the urge to thwack her cousin upon his balding pate. "And if I were not, your almost daily admonitions would ensure that I did not ever forget."

Another wave of empathy for her plight engulfed Pierce.

"Impudent chit. I can turn you out. Just like that, poor relation or not." Fairfax snapped his fingers, and she crimped her mouth tighter, though her eyes railed her outrage.

What a monumental sot, airing Miss Salisbury's reduced status publically like that.

"And do not think I shan't," Fairfax said before seizing his brandy glass and gulping the remains.

Pembroke swore beneath his breath and gave the girl a compassionate smile. He adored nothing better than rescuing a damsel in distress. Well, truth to tell, he liked wooing them more, but not proper young women of station. They expected marriage, and Pembroke had an aversion to the state.

A movement behind the baron drew Pierce's attention.

Arms crossed and leaning one shoulder against the silk-covered wall, Victor, the Duke of Sutcliffe, scowled his displeasure. Because of Victor's raven hair, swarthy coloring, and unusual height, people often mistook him and Pierce as relatives.

Connected to Pierce's three older half-sisters—*the darling, meddlesome trio*—on their mother's side, Victor was the closest thing to a brother Pierce could claim. Besides the brethren of the earls' club, of course.

A few short strokes later, Fairfax placed the still damp I.O.U. in the middle of the table.

Her face, a composed mask of porcelain perfection, and her pretty mouth a narrow, disapproving rose-tinted ribbon, Miss Salisbury glared daggers at Pierce. Gone was the supplication, replaced by accusation and condemnation.

What did she expect him to do?

Cede to Fairfax?

It wasn't done. Surely she understood that.

Chin notched higher yet, and shoulders rigid enough to crack bricks on, she stepped away from her cousin. With majestic grace—and a slight limp?—she retreated to a gold brocade upholstered bench along the wall a few feet from Victor. As if she could not abide watching the game played out but couldn't bear to leave either. Spine sword-straight and every bit as inflexible, she sank gracefully onto the cushion and presented her profile.

Again, that dastardly tender feeling bubbled behind Pierce's ribs, and once more, he squelched it. He couldn't harbor empathy for her and still purpose to crush Fairfax. Such double-mindedness would not do at all.

She complicated matters, and Pierce did not like complications.

Drumming his fingertips atop his cards, he cocked his head as if considering Fairfax's offer, then reached inside his coat and withdrew a stack of notes.

"I'll raise you another twenty thousand."

Except for the purplish veins lacing his nose, the color drained from Fairfax's face, leaving him pallid as death. Fumbling about, he fished his less than pristine handkerchief from his pocket, then mopped his forehead and upper lip. His frenzied gaze swung around the room, sweeping past his cousin, and then jerked back to rest upon her.

His bulgy eyes rounded farther and farther until they dominated his face.

The candlelight accenting her russet hair, she met his gaze head-on, denunciation fairly sparking in her luminous eyes.

Cunning deepened the grooves bracketing Fairfax's mouth.

"By Jove." He flailed his soiled kerchief. "I shall wager the gel, too."

2

Pierce almost put his pointer finger in his ear and shook his head to make sure he had heard correctly.

The baron just said he would stake his cousin, had he not?

Poor wretched girl.

Slowly filling his lungs with air, Pierce peaked an eyebrow in challenge as he contemplated a solution to this unforeseen impediment. Winning a young female most certainly did not fit into his scheme.

Fairfax's loony grin suggested he'd discovered the most brilliant of solutions.

Miss Salisbury's jaw went slack for an instant

before she marshaled her composure and attended to folding her fan, then smoothed her already wrinkle-free, ugly as Hade's skirts.

Such courage she displayed. No histrionics, waterworks, or fainting. Nonetheless, betrayal registered in her eyes before she averted her troubled gaze.

The first indication of meekness Pierce had observed in her.

But then again, she'd just received a monumental blow with a great deal more finesse and comportment than any other female of his acquaintance would've done. And that included the unflappable threesome who flitted about this very ball somewhere. They believed it their duty to interfere in his life with the least provocation on an annoyingly regular basis.

A self-satisfied smile pulled Fairfax's mouth high on one side, revealing two missing teeth, and the others yellowed to the same hue as the Sauce Isigny covering Pierce's asparagus at dinner last night.

"Why, if a man can sell his wife, assuredly I can barter my ward," Fairfax justified.

A buzz of shocked whispers swept those circling the table, and Pembroke and Benton straightened abruptly in their chairs.

Fairfax's last callous remark ratcheted Pierce's abhorrence up several notches.

"Surely such a thing cannot be legal," a woman exclaimed *sotto voce*, a trifle too animated to be truly appalled.

"If he's her guardian," a male chimed in, his voice holding more than a tinge of lasciviousness, "he can do with her what he wishes."

Curse me if that isn't the god-awful truth.

Like a bauble or trinket Fairfax no longer needed or a horse he'd grown tired of.

"I shouldn't mind *at all* if Lord Wainthorpe won me," a sultry feminine voice murmured.

That sounded very much like the not-so-very-long-ago widowed Lady Odette Crutchley. She often hinted she would welcome an arrangement with Pierce. In fact, as recently as the Colfields' rout last week, she'd cornered him on the terrace. A Covent-Garden courtesan couldn't have been bolder or made more vulgar suggestions about how they might further their acquaintance.

She'd not been happy when Pierce had less than cordially declined. He might prefer to dally with experienced women, but not ones who possessed no discretion whatsoever. Besides, she harbored a fondness for opium, had birthed two bastards by separate sires and was rumored to carry the clap.

"The gel's worth at least thirty pounds." Warming to his foul notion, Fairfax bobbed his head.

Miss Salisbury's pert chin edged upward the merest bit, and molten topaz sparks spewed from her eyes.

Pierce masked his disgust behind a mocking smile. Her cousin put a high price on her. He would give him that much. "The gel?"

He knew full well whom the baron meant but wanted to hear him say it. Miss Salisbury needed to hear her cousin speak the words, to realize the peril she was in. She would understand Pierce's actions then.

Probably a stretch there. She might forgive him. Eventually.

Fairfax waggled his pudgy fingers in Miss

Salisbury's direction, careful to avoid eye- contact. Good thing too, because the glare she leveled him would've eviscerated an elephant with one lash.

"Bianca Salisbury, my ward and second cousin once removed. Or is it third cousin?" Fairfax sent her an inquiring glance and received a steely stare in return.

"You don't know *how* she's related to you?"

Fairfax shrugged. "'Tis something along those lines. Distant relation of some sort. I do know she's a direct descendent of James II, and she knows how to manage a household and an estate, too. The chit's a bluestocking through and through, though. Always has her nose in a book or news sheet. Never been to Town before." He winked and gave another cunning, sideways smile. "Innocent of the ways of the world, if you take my meaning."

The buffoon made no effort to lower his voice, and more than one debaucher ogled her with renewed interest.

"If Wainthorpe doesn't accept your offer, Fairfax, I would be interested in negotiating something," one cur had the ballocks to dare, and Lady Crutchley burst into snide laughter.

Pierce yanked his head up to see what devil's spawn made the remark. Three of London's seediest peers openly leered at Miss Salisbury. Devil fly away with them.

What did they think this was?

A perverse game?

Where did they think they were?

A house of ill-repute or a Cyprian Ball?

Miss Salisbury's attention remained riveted on the baron's back, but white lines framed her pinched mouth. There was not a doubt she'd heard them.

Such poise and fortitude.

Blast Pierce's eyes if he wasn't impressed. Such a woman might be worth getting to know.

Several ladies exchanged fervent whispers behind their fans, and he doubted their hushed conversations were complimentary. Why didn't any of these pillars of society rise to Miss Salisbury's defense? Intervene and object to this fiasco?

His sisters would've done, and for once, he would've appreciated their meddling.

No one expected him or the other rogues to champion Miss Salisbury. After all, notorious ne're do wells didn't make a habit of rescuing maidens in distress. But wasn't there one person amongst this peacocking, propriety-touting assembly whose sense of morality and respectability—common decency for that matter—demand they defend her?

Fairfax leaned forward, his tone more wheedling than congenial. "Not bad to look upon, but she's too skinny for my taste." He bowled his hands against his chest, and jostling them, winked again. "Though she's plenty well-endowed where it counts, *eh*?"

"Hear, hear," a crass scoundrel called.

Sweet Jesus on the sacred cross.

Such repugnance engulfed Pierce that he curled his toes and gritted his teeth to keep from reaching across the table and grabbing the baron by his bloody throat. Then proceed to shake the mongrel until he passed out. Maybe Pierce would plant the other disrespectful sods a facer too. All of them for daring to look upon Miss Salisbury with anything other than the deference due a gently-bred woman of her station.

A direct descendent of James II, to boot.

Instead, Pierce turned his full regard to her.

Desperation and humiliation pooled in her eyes, now darkened to the hue of twilight in autumn. Her gaze never wavered from his, and although she spoke not a word, he heard her unspoken plea for aide across the room. Silently beseeching a man she didn't know to help her.

Compassion scraped away at the impenetrable wall he fortified himself behind.

In that instant, he determined to use whatever means necessary, fair or foul, to remove her from Fairfax's clutches. It was pure purgatory to be a woman with no resources, to be at the mercy of a libertine such as her cousin.

Pierce knew what the bugger was capable of. Had witnessed his cruelty firsthand. The baron's kind picked battles with women and children but scuttled off like a frightened insect when confronted with an opponent his equal.

Time to put an end to this.

"I'll accept your wager," Pierce said, still observing

her.

Disbelief, then momentary anguish flashed in her eyes.

He tapped the I.O.U. "Add her as guarantee to our bet. Make no conditions either, or I shan't accept your proposition."

The words fell from Pierce's tongue without conscious thought.

Miss Salisbury's eyes rounded, then shrank to gauging cinnamon slivers.

"Agreed. That is, *if* you win, Wainthorpe. Which is unlikely as purple snow falling tonight." As Fairfax pulled the foolscap toward him and scribbled away, he didn't once glance in Miss Salisbury's direction.

Pierce accepted the sheet and swiftly perused the amendment. He searched Fairfax's confident features. "You didn't assign her guardianship over to me? Should I be victorious, I would expect my ward to depart with me tonight."

"I'm telling you, there's no need." Blowing out a heavy breath, the baron only emphasized the mutiny lining his florid face. "This is all moot, as you shall see in a few moments."

"Humor me anyway." Pierce pushed the foolscap across the table, but the baron simply glowered at him.

As did his cousin.

"Do it, or the bet is off." Pierce leaned back and crossed his arms to prevent himself from glancing at her.

His face contorted into a mutinous scowl, Fairfax seized the paper once more. "If you insist."

"I do."

Fairfax was not exactly known for his scruples or honesty. If the provision was not in writing, it would be difficult for Pierce to press his claim, and Miss Salisbury must be removed from her cousin's custody tonight.

She wasn't safe with the blackguard.

With obvious reluctance, the baron added a couple of lines and, when he finished, held the marker up. "Will that do?"

Pierce perused the sheet, not at all certain of the legality. Still, he was buying Miss Salisbury a little time, if nothing else. "Yes."

"For the love of God, you cannot be serious?" Something more than irritation and chagrin made Miss Salisbury's words rough around the edges.

Fright? Dread?

The notion churned and festered in Pierce's middle. No woman ever had reason to fear him before. That this intriguing creature he would like to become further acquainted with should be the first, caused an unpleasant stirring to swirl behind his breastbone.

Fairfax twisted to look at her and had the audacity to wink.

Her upper lip curled the merest bit.

"You needn't kick up a dust or look so affronted, Bianca. 'Tis just a business transaction." He puffed out his thick chest and jabbed a thumb at his sternum just above a droplet of dried gravy. "I know what I'm doing. You shall see. Soon enough, you'll be pestering me for funds for fripperies and fallalls."

"I have never *pestered* you, nor would I ever do so for nonsensical accouterments." Her body taut and her face wan— a mask of controlled dignity—Miss Salsbury slowly stood. "You shall find, gentlemen, I am not as malleable or witless as you presume if you think I shall willing be a party to this madness."

Pierce cleared his throat, the sound drawing the firebrand's scathing scrutiny.

"Miss Salisbury, I should like to speak with you after the game is at an end. Where might I find you?"

"Well, I shan't be holding court with a bevy of beaux, that's for certain." Her witty retort under dire circumstances earned his admiration.

Demonstrating commendable poise, Miss Salisbury released a despairing little laugh. After giving Pierce a look that could only be described as profound disappointment—a glance that tunneled straight to his gut and twisted the organs with clawed talons—she quit the room.

And yes, though it was barely discernable, she favored one side, making her gait slightly uneven.

Never before had such self-recrimination harangued Pierce.

Yet what choice had he?

Fairfax must be made to pay.

Guests, their expressions avid, swung their

attention between Pierce and Fairfax, almost frothing in their eagerness to see the game's outcome.

Hard to tell which man they preferred to win. Neither was a society favorite.

Waving his cards, Fairfax fairly beamed. "Do you really think I'm daft enough to wager Elmswood and Bianca if I wasn't positive I had you beat, Wainthorpe?"

He chuckled loudly, but the perspiration beading his upper lip belied his humor and bravado.

Pierce was not so much of a scoundrel that he would let Miss Salisbury remain with her wretch of a cousin. Fairfax had stepped well beyond propriety's mark, offering her up like a prized piece of horseflesh. And if he did it once, he would do so again. Only next time, some unscrupulous lout might very well despoil her.

Or worse yet, Fairfax might prostitute her.

Those pointed talons gripped Pierce's innards harder and gave a vicious twist.

No. An inconceivable notion.

He must protect her.

Except for that guardianship business. That

arrangement would never do long-term. He determined long ago to never be responsible for another soul.

He knew just how to deal with that obstacle. Yes, indeed.

Pierce would turn his new ward's care over to the trio.

Surely one of his endearing, interfering sisters would take on the guardianship or find a respectable position for the girl. Why among the three, they boasted nearly a dozen offspring. Mayhap an energetic niece or nephew needed a governess. Yes, just the thing for a bluestocking, and Miss Salisbury wouldn't have to fret about her virtue any longer.

He grazed his hand across his chin, mindful Pembroke and Benton regarded him with unusual scrutiny.

Pierce might as well provide her a purse for a new wardrobe too. As his ward, he couldn't have Miss Salisbury trudging about in gowns as unsightly as that frightening frock she wore tonight. She would look resplendent in deep green—his favorite color—or violet, even saffron.

Perhaps a simple necklace and earrings too. Topaz or pearls or emeralds against her ivory skin?

Did she ride? Like the theater?

Perhaps dancing and French lessons were in order as well.

What if gentlemen wanted to call upon her?

Should Pierce permit it?

That notion rested in his gut as unpleasantly as tainted oysters.

Way ahead of yourself there, old chap.

Enough woolgathering.

Tend to the task at hand.

Pierce poured himself another dram of brandy. He seldom indulged in more than two drinks. That he did so tonight launched the other two members of the Wicked Earls' Club eyebrows high onto their noble foreheads.

Curiosity every bit as acute as the guests' danced in their eyes. But they would respect his privacy just as he respected theirs. At least until they were assembled within the club's sacred walls.

By no means could the same be said of Victor.

His glower deepened further, but at least he held his tongue. He would save his lecture for when he and Pierce were alone. And given the darkling look he sliced Pierce, a lengthy monologue, chock-full of chastisements, could be expected. Most especially when it came to accepting Fairfax's cousin as a stake in a wager.

Likely, with the exception of the other wicked earls and Victor, everyone else present—including the stormy-eyed Miss Salisbury—thought Pierce did so because he was an incorrigible, immoral degenerate.

But he meant to save her from a debased cur. Fairfax.

"Let's see your hand then." Pierce made a pretense of feigning dire interest.

His smug smile stretched wide, Fairfax splayed his cards. "Trump flush."

The onlookers let out an appreciative rumble.

"Oh, I say. Well done."

"Ain't every day you see that."

"Oh, I do believe the baron has won," a woman trilled.

Only one combination was better.

A rare hand and one Pierce had only seen dealt once before.

Smiling like a foxed rhesus monkey, Fairfax leaned forward, prepared to scoop the winnings into his sweaty palms.

Hooking his ankle over his knee and slinging an arm across the back of his chair, Pierce hitched his mouth into an I've-got-you-now-you-bloody-sot-grin before flipping over the top card, the ace facing upward atop the ten-point.

"Pam-flush."

Fairfax wheezed in alarm.

Pierce tapped the knave of clubs once with his forefinger. "I win."

3

Bianca tore toward the lady's retiring room. A cold sweat dribbled down her spine, and her blood careened through her veins. She'd meant to be brave and strong, to stay and witness the outcome. But when Bertram signed over her guardianship to a stranger…

That betrayal had been too much. Too degrading.

If only she could've disappeared, not seen the mixture of expressions turned toward her: pity, calculation, lasciviousness, satisfaction, embarrassment, and more.

She swallowed, truly fearful she might cast up her accounts. A loud buzzing in her ears and her knees gone to jelly proved equally worrisome. Was this what it felt like when one was about to swoon? Inconvenient to succumb to such feminine weakness for the first time, to be sure.

She darted into an alcove. With an undignified *whomp*, she plumped onto the smallish settee within and bent forward, her head dangling between her knees. More hair escaped the simple knot she'd contrived before the small looking glass of her rented room, just larger than the kitchen larder at Elmswood.

Breathing slowly and deeply, inhaling to a count of ten and then exhaling to another count of ten, she willed the faintness to pass. A couple of minutes later, she lifted her head a few inches and waited, her senses on tenterhooks.

A bit better.

At least the room ceased spinning like a child's freshly wound top.

It wouldn't do to keel over, adding more fodder to the scandal that already blazed around Bianca. She took a moment to rub her sore ankle. She'd twisted it earlier, aggravating an old break. Aunt Florencia said Bianca had broken it as a toddler, and the bone had failed to heal correctly. Bianca didn't remember the injury, and except for an occasional ache, she forgot about her slightly turned-out foot.

Slipping from the nook, she wiped a shaky palm across her forehead and then turned the corner, discovering a set of stairs. Normally, her nerves were steady as a sea captain's march across his pitching ship's deck, but the ludicrousness below had befuddled her. One hand pressed to her middle, and the other clenching her skirts and fan, she sucked in a fortifying gulp of air as she dashed up the risers.

God help her.

Bertram had used her as collateral in a wager with an infamous rakehell. A man whose sullied reputation garnered a stern warning away from him her second day in London. A lord who now, at least on that vile slip of paper, might've become her guardian.

"God help me," she muttered aloud this time.

Meet him afterward indeed. Was he a complete beef wit?

According to several peeresses and prestigious dames, if he and the motley crew he kept company with didn't hold titles, they'd never be accepted in polite company. Nevertheless, the younger set—specifically marriageable-age females—held those privileged banes of society in an entirely different light.

Seems the *ton* looked the other direction when it came to peers of the realms' indiscretions. A shortage of eligible, title-bearing men and a bevy of young damsels and their husband-hunting mothers contributed to that forgiving attitude.

Not so for pockets-to-let country misses whose only relative bartered her away like a hairy Highland cow. Even if Bianca *was* a descendent of James II.

A wave of fury billowed over her, so potent her head spun again. She shut her eyes and clutched at the banister until it passed.

Another disturbing thought struck, and her eyes popped wide open.

In all of Grand Uncle Sylvester's library and study, she'd never come across anything, not even a family Bible, to prove the ancestral connection to James II. A long ago relative, eager to impress, might very well have made the tale up. And then the nonsense had been passed down generation after generation as factual.

Thank God, thus far, no one had challenged the assertion.

What the devil would she do if they did?

That claim was the only respectable thing she possessed to use as leverage for gaining employment. Something she must find at once, no thanks to Bertram.

Bertram.

The worm. Maggot. Horse turd.

So was the dratted Earl of Wainthorpe.

In the card room, every muscle tensed, Bianca had held her breath. Features arranged into blandness, she prayed over and over that Lord Wainthorpe possessed the smallest shred of decency somewhere in his tarnished soul. That the too attractive earl would rebuff Bertram's preposterous proposal.

But rather than muster an iota of honor, the devilishly handsome lord, with his high cheekbones and strong chin, coolly assessed her with those olive dark discs. Then had the gall to stipulate she must go with him if he won.

Tonight.

And Bertram had agreed.

In front of half of London.

Wainthorpe was as rotten a cur as her cousin. His soul blacker than his shiny raven hair.

So why had her silly pulse quickened each time he'd turned his unusual jet gaze on her? And why did she wish she wore a fine gown and jewels? Wanted her hair beautifully arranged in a fashion similar to the other women watching the game?

Surely the earl realized accepting such a wager relegated her to the same status as demimondaine or a kept woman. She was not so naive as to think he meant to employ her as a housekeeper or secretary. Whoever heard of a female clerk or a housekeeper not beyond their fortieth summer?

No, Wainthorpe knew full well what he was about, and yet without as much as a glint of remorse, he collaborated to ruin her. A stranger to him.

What sort of unconscionable cur did that?

Except, what about that guardianship provision?

Might that make a difference?

Make the awfulness slightly more acceptable? Respectable even?

Probably not. The gossips wouldn't care about that detail.

Resuming her ascent, Bianca drew her eyebrows together into a fierce frown. From the instant she first gazed upon Bertram last year, she'd sensed something off about him. Still, she strove to make the best of the situation.

Because... Well, the truth of the matter was, she *was* the poor relation.

Elmswood had been her home for a decade, since she was almost ten. After her mum died, she came to live with her childless Grand Uncle Sylvester and Grand Aunt Florencia. They were Mum's only living relatives, and they'd also taken Mum in when her parents had died of cholera.

Florencia had died over seven years ago, and Bianca now wore her remade gown. From her aunt's old clothes and a pair of bed curtains, she'd fashioned a wardrobe, as well as saved money by stitching her own garments.

Before coming to London, she'd been proud of her self-taught seamstress skills.

Until she saw the gorgeous ensembles worn by the elite ladies of the *ton,* that is. Such lovely, delicate fabrics and lace. Such flattering colors and fits. All those brilliant ribbons, bows, sashes, and fallalls.

Bianca glanced down and grimaced.

She looked exactly like what she was.

A frumpy country dowd come to town.

Clothes were never a matter of concern before. But a small part of her, that feminine portion that cherished pretty, lacy things, longed for a gown half as exquisite as those she saw others parading about in. When the earl had taken her measure, his midnight brow twitching the tiniest bit as he took in her ensemble, humiliation had heated her cheeks.

Nothing for it though. She would not cringe in chagrin or shame either. She couldn't spare coin to purchase a new wardrobe in any event. Especially not now.

Bianca's meager savings wouldn't last a month in London.

Since no man showed any marked interest in paying his addresses, she must find a position, post haste. Her unpopular coloring, clothing far below the first sprig of fashion, and a lack of dowry played major roles. She wasn't terribly surprised. Or terribly disappointed, for that matter.

Till now, Bianca had been content at Elmswood Parke. Part of Aunt Florencia's marriage settlement, she and Uncle Sylvester preferred the manor to his other two entailed estates.

These past few months, Bianca realized Bertram cared nothing about the place. Except for what he could extract from the estate monetarily. It wouldn't be long until he brought them to destitution, and then he would sell the unentailed property.

She felt sure of it.

No amount of talking or reasoning made an impression on him. Hard-headed and stiff-necked, he dismissed her concerns. Almost always accompanied by threats to turn her onto the street if she didn't mind her tongue and her own business.

She hadn't anywhere to go. So she stifled her comments and kept her fretting to herself until his next despicable act. In the meanwhile, she'd plotted how to ensure her future.

By appealing to his vanity and warped sense of importance, Bianca had persuaded Bertram to allow her to accompany him to London for the Season. He hinted he sought a bride—a wealthy bride. If she were a little long in the tooth, he didn't mind as long as her settlement portion proved substantial. He sincerely believed his title was all he needed to achieve that lofty goal.

Bianca was honest enough to acknowledge there was some small truth to that, in fact.

She'd convinced him that, with her by his side, he might ascend to *le beau monde's* upper salons more readily and therefore have access to more potential Lady Fairfaxes. Her pristine heritage did indeed open doors, not that she anticipated something as frivolous as a

Come Out for herself.

No, much more practical needs motivated her. But now, on her cousin's whim, she had been gambled away. An expendable commodity.

Surely Bertram and his lordship suspected she would refuse to cooperate.

What did the earl think?

Bianca would meekly follow him to his carriage like one of his Cyprians?

Oh, how she longed to box his ears, the dunderhead.

I say, your lordship. My reputation is of no import. Do with me what you will.

She refused to acknowledge the little tingle of excitement the thought stirred.

Lord Wainthorpe was a rapscallion. A knave of the worst sort

Then why did her blood hum through her veins with something other than pure vexation?

Murmurs about his pedigree abounded, too. Young ladies proved a tremendous source of fascinating information when they thought no one was listening nearby. Bianca often sat in a corner or stood beside a festooned window, unnoticed and forgotten, and learned the most indecorous things.

How the earl had been orphaned and came into his title at eight years old. How he never set foot in England until then and refused to speak English for the first six months. How he claimed royalty through his Indian heritage that surpassed a mere English earldom.

His lineage had failed to mold him into a man of noble character, to be certain.

Her stomach flopped sickeningly.

Won by a wicked earl.

She drew in a long, soothing breath and slowly released it through pursed lips.

No sense getting into a complete dither. Yet.

Wainthorpe mightn't have won the game. Bertram might've prevailed, she reassured herself in an attempt to steady her hammering heart. The irregular cadence was surely caused by upset and high emotion rather than unnerving ponderings on what the earl intended to do with her.

It mattered naught.

She couldn't—*wouldn't*—reside with Bertram any longer.

He'd shown the corrupt depths he was capable of sinking to, and if the Earl of Wainthorpe failed to win the hand after all, Bertram might very well try to barter her again.

Now what for all of England's love of tea *was* she to do?

Bianca would sprout a tail and wings before submitting to Bertram's whims anymore. Yet, she wasn't of age for another eleven months, and because she'd lived an isolated life at Elmswood Parke, she claimed no close female acquaintances she might live with.

At the upper landing, she paused to gather her bearings.

Women's muffled laughter carried to her from farther along the passageway. As she made her way down the corridor, solemn-faced nobility stared down upon her from their gilded frames. These past weeks, she had made a few casual friends, but certainly no one she could impose upon to take her in.

Drawing another bolstering breath, she pushed the latch to the lady's retiring room. Four ladies occupied the chamber, none of whom she was acquainted with.

A striking brunette, perhaps in her fifth decade, sat before a mirror and applied rice powder. Another woman greatly resembling her perched in a chair, mending a tear in her hem. A third woman, slightly younger with fairer hair and the same unusual pale green eyes, lounged on a settee while a fourth applied rouge to her already ruby-tinted lips.

Each glanced at the entrance when Bianca opened the door, and she managed a small smile.

"Oh, you poor, dear woman," the lip rouge miss gushed, her mouth tipped into a sympathetic smile.

Perfectly grand.

The girl must've been in or near the card room. Else the gossip made the rounds in spectacular time.

Bianca's smile slipped, but she entered the chamber regardless.

Better the foursome than the crowd of clucking hens and posturing roosters below. And this quartet would eventually leave, so she might have a few moments to contemplate what to do.

Unless more guests paraded in.

Perhaps she ought to have sought refuge in the library or study. Or even a garden arbor.

Too late now.

"What makes you say such a provocative thing, Miss Walcott?" asked the woman tending to her hem. She paused in stitching the loose lace on her spring green and ivory gown to give Miss Walcott an acute stare.

"Indeed?" the brunette asked, her tone somewhat starchier.

It appeared they didn't hold Miss Walcott in the highest regard.

"You haven't heard yet?" Her big brown, pansy eyes wide and blameless, Miss Walcott faced Bianca. "Silly me. *Of course* you haven't. How could you possibly have done? Why, I only know because I was there. And it's only been but fifteen minutes at most," she blathered.

If ten minutes had passed yet, Bianca would dance a one-legged jig.

Miss Walcott dimpled again, and Bianca was hard-pressed to determine if the girl was perpetually cheery, truly concerned, or just eager to share the tattle.

Might as well grab the goose by its tail feathers, as Uncle Sylvester used to say.

"I assume you're referring to my cousin offering me as a stake in his card game?" Bianca looked at each lady in turn.

The three ladies' eyes rounded in astonishment, and they exchanged incredulous glances. Something about the planes of the older two women's faces, something with their cheeks and jaw lines, reminded her of Wainthorpe. It must be their striking coloring.

Wariness tinged the elder's face, and the edges of her mouth grew hard.

"That's utterly barbaric and far beyond the pale," she said, snapping her compact shut. "I'd better not be acquainted with any of the participants to that farce, I'll tell you. They'll get a piece of my mind that will have their ears ringing until next Season! Just see if I'm home to them after this."

"What kind of blackguard would agree to such a despicable thing?" The woman attired in shades of soft pink and relaxing on the settee fidgeted with a curl near her ear. "No one of our acquaintance, surely, would have a heart that evil."

As she twisted the cap back on the rouge jar, Miss Walcott's smile became even more syrupy, and she peaked her brows in a superior fashion. "I was indeed referring to *that* wager."

A chinwag then, and so young too. A pity, really.

"I must say, I was beyond appalled." Miss Walcott appeared nothing of the sort. Gleeful was more apt a description.

Apparently, she was the type of gossip who liked to draw out a tale, reveling in the false sense of self-importance that being privy to *on dit* afforded her. She chose to ignore the other ladies' questions, too. That decision said much of her, and Bianca found it oddly disappointing.

Miss Walcott *tsked* her sympathy as disingenuous as the paste diamonds circling her milky-white throat. "You're a most *unfortunate* woman."

Bianca hid her wince at Miss Walcott's innuendo. Even she knew an unfortunate woman referred to a prostitute. The inference stung acutely.

"Miss Walcott! That's outside of enough and beneath you." Again the eldest woman jumped to Bianca's defense.

"Oh, do stop stirring up a dust, Lady Timberly," Miss Walcott said while donning her gloves.

Impudent bit of fluff, isn't she?

"I only meant her circumstance is quite intolerable. Is it not?" she asked. "Why if it were me, I'm quite sure I'd be weeping hysterically or having a fit of the vapors."

"Well, she's not you. She has the good sense to keep her wits about her in a vexing situation. Well done you, miss," the lady attired in pink declared as she levered herself upright and gave an approving nod.

Acutely aware Miss Walcott and the others observed her progress, Bianca made her way to a table with glasses, pitchers of lemonade and ratafia, and a decanter of sherry. She would like a nip of Uncle Sylvester's Drambuie, but if the Scottish liquor graced any *haute ton* drinking cabinets, she would quack like a duck. She poured herself a half glass of too-sweet lemonade and, after taking a long drink, faced the women once more.

Curiosity fairly oozed from them, yet only Miss Walcott dared to pursue the topic.

"Whatever will you do?" she asked.

Bianca lifted a shoulder as she tucked a plaguy strand behind her ear. She was not about to disclose her fears to strangers. Besides, she didn't yet know what she would do. No brilliant plan had sprung to mind in the past two minutes.

"You needn't fret on my account." She set the glass aside. "I'm remarkably resourceful." Something impish gripped her, and she swept her hand down the front of her gown. "Would you believe I made this myself? From a cast-off, too."

Clamping her teeth together, she checked her giggle at the comical expressions flitting across the women's faces as they tried to summon an appropriate, polite reply.

Perhaps a bit dense, Miss Walcott frowned, her forehead furrowed into three even rows. "*You* made your…*erm*…gown?"

"I did." Bianca smiled wider, mischief prodding her on. "I have the most unusual riding habit too. A dark brown affair made from my dead grand uncle's bed curtains. I used the tie-backs to adorn the collar and sleeves."

Agog, the four women stared.

It really was too bad of her. Still, Bianca couldn't resist.

"Want to know what I made my undergarments from?" Mouth curved, all guileless innocence, she gave them an inquisitive glance. "Bed linens."

Miss Walcott blinked faster. "Wh—"

"Most resourceful of you." The lady wearing green beamed before spearing the blonde beauty a glare guaranteed to strike her mute.

The striking brunette stood and offered a genuine smile. "Allow me to introduce myself. I know 'tis not *de rigueur*, but since there are only the four of us…"

Probably desperate to change the topic away from Bianca's horror of a gown. Or what she sewed her underthings from.

"I am Viscountess Lenora Timberly." She arced her hand at the other two ladies. "These are my sisters, Mrs. Rebecca Garside." *The lady in green.* "And Amanda, the Countess of Mulbrury." *The one in pink.* "And she," Lady Timberly barely wiggled her forefinger toward the animated Miss Walcott, "is Miss Daisy Walcott."

Daisy?

Oh dear, no. No.

The name didn't suit at all.

In fact, it was a disservice to Aunt Florencia's long-dead, sweet-tempered Pomeranian that bore the same moniker.

Rose better befitted Miss Walcott. Beautiful, but also given to unexpectedly pricking. Perhaps even scratching and drawing blood.

The quartet regarded Bianca with acute interest, and she collected her wayward musings.

"A pleasure." She dipped into an agile curtsy. "I am Bianca Salisbury."

She'd heard of Lady Timberly and her sisters, though she had not met them. Well-regarded and influential, and if tattle were true, kind. But also proper down to the last curl on their perfectly coiffed heads.

If only they would take their leave.

Precious little time remained for Bianca to contrive a plan. With a short, dismissive nod—hopefully they would take the hint—she skirted the couch and, after taking a seat at one of the tables, set about re-pinning her hair. The mass possessed a mind of its own, and wayward curls frequently crept loose of their confines.

She inherited her Scottish father's hair, Aunt Florencia often declared. A shade somewhere between auburn and coffee. Too bad Bianca didn't know any of her Salisbury relatives or traipsing to Scotland to escape her current humiliation would've been an option.

Even after Mum died of some sort of internal affliction and Bianca came to live with her aunt and uncle, no one mentioned Papa. Except on the rare occasions when Aunt Florencia was in her cups. Uncle Sylvester usually shushed her straightaway and hustled her to bed to sleep off her over-indulgence.

On one such occasion, she revealed that Papa hailed from a prominent Scots family in Aberdeen and that Bianca's mum fell madly in love with him. A mere three weeks after meeting at a house party—Mum just sixteen and Papa one and twenty—they'd eloped to Italy, of all places.

Which explained Bianca's Italian name, for she'd been conceived there.

Done primping, Miss Walcott sat on the settee's arm. She dangled one leg, revealing the exquisitely embroidered satin slipper encasing her dainty foot.

Fighting the urge to glance at her own rather large feet attired in practical, unadorned black shoes, Bianca caught sight of Lady Timberly regarding her in the mirror.

"Miss Salisbury—"

"Don't you want to know who accepted Lord Fairfax's wager?" Miss Walcott all but chirped, revealing those two adorable dimples again and practically bouncing with the news she couldn't wait to share.

Must she be so dashed bubbly?

Bianca found she couldn't quite dislike the merry girl, despite her propensity for rumormongering.

Three pairs of perplexed gazes traveled to Miss Walcott.

"Who? Or is it whom?" Mrs. Garside snipped off the thread and, once she set the needle aside, stood and shook out her skirt. She looked to her sisters. "Are we acquainted with a Lord Fairfax?"

Shaking her head, Lady Timberly leveled Miss Walcott a stern look. "I don't believe so. And Miss Walcott, I shall remind you since you seem to have forgotten your manners. 'Tis impolite to interrupt and even poorer form to spread tales."

Crossing her arms, Miss Walcott formed a moue with her rosebud mouth.

"Well, I can understand why *you* would want to keep everything *hush-hush* since it was *your* brother who won her."

everal insistent raps upon his bedchamber door dragged Pierce from his exhaustion-induced slumber. The half bottle of brandy he imbibed after searching for Miss Salisbury—unsuccessfully—until three this morning might be a contributing factor to the unpleasant burnt peat taste in his mouth and the thunder resonating inside his skull.

With a groan, he turned his head and forced a weighty eyelid open to peek at the bedside clock.

He squinted and blinked three times to focus his blurry vision.

Seven of the clock.

Blister and blast. Seven?

No wonder he felt like a coach and four had plowed him over. Twice. He'd only slept two hours. With another groan, caused more by the hammer cracking the inside of his skull than the beating upon his door, he pulled a pillow over his head.

"Go 'way."

Deuce it all.

What could Popplewell be thinking?

Pierce rose at eight. *Eight.* Not Seven.

And his man never entered the chamber a minute prior unless explicitly requested to do so. When Poppelwell did arrive, he bore strong, steaming Turkish coffee and was followed by footmen bearing hot water for Pierce's morning soak.

He did not bang upon the blasted door like oxen learning the *tabla* drums.

Sighing, Pierce tossed the pillow aside.

He was awake now.

The same thought he'd drifted asleep to crowded into the forefront of his tortured head.

Where is Miss Bianca Salisbury?

He'd lost his new ward—within hours of being appointed her guardian, too.

Something very near to shame engulfed Pierce for a moment, and he pressed two fingers to his closed eyes.

Not a trace did he find of her. He'd intended to explain himself to her immediately after winning, but she vanished. With over a hundred people milling about, she simply disappeared as if spirited away by an *apsaras*. A fairy.

A couple more knocks shook the door, earning the carved walnut a fuming glare.

What the devil was Popplewell about?

Or…?

Had someone dared to impose themselves on Pierce's household at this wholly unacceptable hour? Which justified his disregarding the scratching and bumping about in the corridor just now. He was *never* at home to guests before the clock struck twelve.

His thoughts circled back to the critical matter at hand, and he smacked a pillow with his fist.

Miss Salisbury's, *Bianca's*, humiliation must be

beyond bearable. He desperately wanted to reassure her and squelch any fears she might have.

Was the transaction … the appointment—whatever the blazes it was called—making her his ward legal? Probably not, and that worried as much as her disappearance. Because Fairfax could demand her return, and the possibility remained that the rotter would prevail in court.

Not without a deuced ugly fight, he wouldn't.

Sucking in a cleansing breath, Pierce uncurled his fingers. The baron would need funds for a solicitor, and according to Pierce's man Churchgrove, Fairfax couldn't cough up a pence at the moment.

What was it about Bianca that brought out Pierce's full-on protective instincts?

Last night, or rather at half-past one in the morning, he rode to the rooms the baron was reported to have rented. In a less than reputable, let alone fashionable, part of London, at that. Of his lordship, Pierce found nary a trace. But a tiny room with an even tinier cot bore evidence of Bianca. Actually, the half dozen poorly sewn gowns draped upon the bed—each impossibly uglier than the last—convinced Pierce he'd located her lodgings.

He swore one atrocious brown rag looked to have been stitched from faded draperies.

But Bianca hadn't returned there.

He pounded the pillow with his fist again.

By Hades, where had she gone?

Part of him wanted to breathe a sigh of relief and say good riddance.

A very trifling part.

He neither wanted nor needed such an encumbrance or responsibility. But the other part, the irrational, annoyingly decent part that insisted he was not quite the uncaring libertine he projected to the world, wouldn't stop worrying about her.

The image of her face, that last wounded glance she'd thrown him, wouldn't leave his memory.

Her eyes.

Those spectacular orbs haunted him.

When Pierce closed his own, he could see the dark

amber shards glittering and stricken. So many emotions warring within their unusual depths.

She'd clearly hoped he would save her by denying the wager, and instead, she believed he'd collaborated with her miscreant of a cousin.

Pierce *had* rescued her.

In a manner of speaking. At least temporarily, until he could have his solicitor poke around the guardianship situation. Only Bianca had vanished. How was Pierce to protect her from the baron and other riffraff if he didn't know where she was?

Still, it appeared Fairfax had scuttled away, for the time being at least. God only knew where he'd gone or when he would slither 'round again.

Pierce intended to be ready if he did. Which meant he probably ought to pry himself off his mattress and send a missive to his solicitor. Only opening his eyes and stirring seemed a Herculean task, most especially without his favored morning brew.

Whispering commenced in the corridor—rather loud feminine whispering—a trice before his door flew open.

What the...?

"Pierce Baxter Maximillian Chamberlain," Lenora chided. "I'd never have thought you capable of such shenanery. I'm truly appalled, Wainthorpe."

Wainthorpe?

Nora never addressed Pierce by his title. She *was* in a proper dither. And for her to invade his bedchamber, appeared to have taken leave of her senses as well.

"Good morning to you too, Lenora."

Pierce cracked an eyelid open, then flopped onto his back and yawned without bothering to cover his mouth. "I must say, I've never known you to depart your chamber before ten. What's the special occasion?"

Resplendent in a dark blue redingote and matching silk bonnet, she frowned her disapproval as she marched to the window and then yanked open the draperies.

Sunbeams, much too cheerful and bright for a May morning in London, spilled into the room.

He squinted against the lancing pain behind his eyes.

No more brandy for him. Ever.

"We," she motioned to the doorway where his other sisters stood, hesitant half-smiles curving their mouths, "surmised our intervention was required when we met dear Miss Salisbury last evening."

"You met her? Do you know where she is then?"

Pierce shot up at once, and the bedcoverings slid to his waist, exposing his naked chest. He sucked in a hissing breath between his teeth and clutched at his exploding head with both hands.

Amanda gasped. "Pierce! For pity's sake. Have you no modesty?"

"None whatsoever, Mandy, and I'll remind you, you are the ones who appeared in my bedchamber at seven in the morning." She was always the easiest to embarrass.

Rebecca snickered as she sank onto a chair. "Are you *completely* nude, brother dearest?"

Pierce cocked a brow in answer, and his most outlandish sister laughed outright.

Lenora spun to face him. Arms akimbo, she shook

her head, though wry amusement ticked her mouth up a jot. "Must you be scandalous *all* of the time?"

"I do try." He gave her a mischievous wink, which softened his eldest sister's disapproval further.

Unsurprisingly, Lenora remained the most proper. Although in her defense, she had assumed the role of mother to her younger sisters when only thirteen. Then years later, Pierce arrived in England: an angry, resentful child, full of hatred for his father's people.

Through love, patience, and a good deal of persistence, she won him over. All of his sisters had, and he remained devoted to them, despite his reputation as an unfeeling rake.

"I was not expecting to entertain company before I shaved and enjoyed a pot of coffee." He rubbed his palm across his stubbly chin. "And I'm honored to think you found the situation so serious that the three of you are at my bedchamber door before the cock crows. I believe that's a first for you all."

With a mocking grin, he yawned again and scratched his chest. He never entertained his few ladyloves at home. His house was his sanctuary. Which is why he rarely ever permitted callers.

Not even the wicked earls, excepting Pembroke and Coventry.

"I wasn't keen on rising before dawn. I'll tell you that." Amanda plopped into the other armchair. She did look rather peaked.

His attention dropped to her middle.

Was she increasing *again*?

That would make five for her.

In consideration of their tender sensibilities, he drew the sheet a trifle higher. "Lenora, pull the bell, and I'll ask Popplewell to bring tea up as well as coffee. And a tray too. I'm assuming none of you have broken your fast?"

"We've already seen to it," Rebecca said. "Although Popplewell and your other staff are in quite a fuss at our arriving on your doorstep at this hour. I truly thought they might refuse us entrance for a moment."

Hardly. No one denied the trio anything.

That worrisome notion wiggled its way into Pierce's mind and took root. He surveyed them, each in turn. They were up to something, and primal instinct shouted he was not going to like it.

Giving Pierce a conspiratorial wink, Rebecca pulled off a glove. "I'm actually rather hungry, and I normally eschew breakfast. Must be the excitement."

"Pierce darling, did you truly win that sweet girl at cards?" Curiosity rather than condemnation pulled Amanda's fine eyebrows together. She settled more comfortably in the armchair and placed a palm on her abdomen.

Yes, most definitely in the family way again.

Covertly eyeing Amanda's belly, Pierce tried to estimate how far along she was.

Not very. She wasn't showing.

He hid a delighted grin behind his hand. He adored babies.

Other people's babies.

It wouldn't do for that weakness to get out. He did have an austere reputation to maintain, after all.

Jaded, hardened, cynical, uncaring. A man about town.

But holding an infant, smelling the babe's sweet essence and listening to its soft breathing—nothing was quite as special. Sacred almost. Of course, when they cried or needed their diapers changed, he promptly returned the child to its doting mother.

"I did win your Miss Salisbury, but the situation isn't quite what you think." A cracking good headache thrummed inside Pierce's skull, and he touched a fingertip to his right temple. The familiar puckered ridge pulsed to the same tempo as the din banging in his head.

"That's perfectly horrid and beneath you, Pierce darling." Lenora's features softened, and she came to stand at the foot of the bed. "What could you have been thinking? I know you feel you must cock-a-snook at society. And I understand why. I truly do. But we know," again she gestured to their sisters, "that you are a truly decent, caring, honorable man despite doing your utmost to convince everyone otherwise."

"I bet he was thinking how beautiful Miss Salisbury

is. Her eyes are the most unusual color. Like spiced, mulled cider. Very alluring. Don't you agree, brother dearest?" Rebecca quipped with an impish grin. "Though I thought you preferred brunettes."

"No, Becca, dear. You're mistaken. That last actress was a blonde." Face a shade paler than it was a moment before, Amanda shook her head. "And the demimondaine before her was too."

For the love of God. How did they know *that*?

Something that felt very much like a flush of chagrin heated Pierce's neck and face.

Apparently, he wasn't discreet enough. Or...had someone spied on him?

No, his sisters wouldn't have given such orders. However, any one of their starchy husbands would've done in a blink. That notion rather stuck in his craw.

"No, no, my dear," Lenora disagreed. "That was the one prior. The voluptuous widow, I believe. She was *not* a natural blonde either. She had dark roots with a few strands of gray."

Her pointer finger on her chin, Lenora had such a

look of concentration on her face that if the situation wasn't so ghastly uncomfortable, Pierce would've laughed.

Time to change the subject before they listed every woman rumored to have been with him. They would be heartily surprised to learn there weren't nearly as many as he led others to believe. The actress was a skilled chess player, and he'd posed—fully clothed—for the widow's sojourn into oil painting.

"You didn't answer my questions. Do you know where my ward is?"

That stopped the trio's conjectures as swiftly as a blast of arctic air up their costly skirts.

"Ward?" they chorused as one, their light peridot eyes huge as their neat eyebrows shot upward.

He did chuckle then. If they practiced their reaction, they couldn't have been more synchronized.

"Yes. *Ward.*" Pierce raked a hand through his hair.

So Bianca had failed to mention that particular tidbit to his sisters.

"Just how foul a man do you take me for? I insisted

Fairfax sign over Miss Salisbury's guardianship. A man like that wouldn't hesitate to barter her again. To prostitute her. I knew I held a winning hand, but I took no chance of him wheedling his way back into her life."

Forehead knitted, Rebecca laid her gloves on the table beside her chair.

"But is that legal? Just to sign over a guardianship like that?" She snapped her fingers.

Pierce hunched a shoulder, then snatched the sheet as it ventured into embarrassing proximity of his hips. "I don't know. Unlikely, I suppose. But I mean to pursue that very issue when I rise. Something I could do more readily if I didn't have you three busybodies in my bedchamber. If you're so keen on propriety, you'll vacate at once."

"I'm sure Mason knows a person or two who might advise you. I shall speak to him the instant I return home." Lenora, too, set about removing her gloves.

Evidently his intrusive sisters intended to stay and eat, too.

Something they'd done when Pierce had first

arrived in England. However, breakfasting in a belligerent boy's chamber was a far cry from doing so in an adult male's. Even if he was their brother.

He speared a glance toward the door.

What the devil was keeping Popplewell?

Amanda, her eyes bright with approval, fairly beamed. "I knew there must be a noble explanation. You were trying to protect Miss Salisbury's honor. Oh, she shall be so relieved."

Only eleven years his senior, she usually championed him.

"So she's safe? You know where she is?" Inexplicable relief encompassed Pierce.

"I'm right here, your lordship."

And Bianca was.

And so was Popplewell, *finally*, as well as Elsie, one of the maids.

"Excuse me, miss." His head angled at a stiff, disapproving angle, Popplewell, followed by Elsie, brushed past Miss Salisbury. They hustled into the chamber and swiftly set about depositing their laden trays.

Bianca wore what must be a borrowed gown. Most likely Rebecca's as she was the tallest of his sisters. The light peach spencer over a mint green gown complemented Bianca's coloring. Soft burnished ringlets framed her face under what could only be described as a charming green bonnet adorned with silk flowers in coral and yellows.

Good Lord, she was stunning. And deliciously tempting.

She looked like a piece of fresh fruit. And Pierce wanted to pluck her from the tree and taste her sweet essence.

Her curious dark honey-toned gaze slowly roved over Pierce's bare chest and shoulders before following the thin trail of dark hair from his abdomen to where it disappeared beneath the sheets. Instead of blushing or looking away as most proper young ladies would've done, she met his gaze and tilted her head, a distinct dare in her bearing.

Was she accustomed to seeing men's naked chests?

No, she might not have averted her hungry gaze, but pink tinged her high cheekbones. She couldn't control the instinctive response, and it provided Pierce a small reprieve to know she was not as unaffected as she pretended.

Still… "My banyan, Popplewell."

Oddly, with her standing in his sister's finery, looking every bit the proper lady, Pierce felt at a disadvantage. With that glorious hair and those equally magnificent eyes, she would shine everyone else down if dressed thusly at an assembly or rout.

Did she suspect his nakedness beneath the bedcovers?

Bold and unflinching, she sank her keen gaze to his lap, and her lush mouth quirked upward. Her cheeks glowed brighter, too

Pierce had never met a woman like her before. One who fascinated him and rattled his senses with a single knowing glance. No false pretense of demureness or offended sensibilities, but most assuredly not the hardened, calculating glint of a woman of loose virtue either.

Zounds. He'd never felt so blasted awkward in his life.

And the trio had never been so silent in all of theirs.

It couldn't be Bianca's warm treacle eyes caressing his skin from across the room causing his disquiet. Or the glimmer of amusement slightly crinkling the corners of her mouth.

It hit him then.

She was enjoying his discomfort. Immensely, if the pleased smile framing her mouth were any indication.

With Popplewell's assistance, Pierce managed to slide his arms into his burgundy robe and close it over his chest without exposing more of his nude form. Sliding a hand through his hair for the third time, he turned his mouth down. Time to take matters in hand and end this preposterousness and invasion into his chamber.

"You really oughtn't to be in my bedchamber, Miss Salisbury. It's most improper. You risk utter ruin."

The slow bowing of her mouth made his nape hair

stand straight on end.

Excitement or trepidation?

For the longest moment, Pierce couldn't force his focus from those coral pink lips. She must've noticed his impolite stare—how could she not?—because her smile widened the merest bit.

She alone possessed the ability to fluster him in a way no other woman had before. It unnerved him. A great deal, truth to tell. Since he was a young lad, he'd stoically controlled his emotions and his responses.

Her mouth curved up a fraction farther, and he gave himself a mental kick in the arse.

Ballocks, he still gawked like a milksop.

Noting his gaffe, she swooped in to verbally pin him to the headboard.

"And you're a perfect model of decorum, my lord?"

Her voice was not low and husky. Still, it held a depth, a melodic richness that made him yearn to hear her talk more.

She touched a finger to her cheek, the movement calculated and coy.

"Or, as my guardian, should I address you as Pierce now?"

Popplewell made an inarticulate noise, which sounded very much like he'd swallowed a whole ham. Teapot in hand, he turned to gape at her in disbelief.

The quick-witted maid rescued the tilting vessel lest the flummoxed servant douse his feet with the scalding brew.

One of Pierce's sisters gasped and another giggled.

He couldn't be sure which did which, for he spared them not a glance. Every part of him was attuned to the mocking, angry beauty mere feet away.

God's bones, Miss Bianca Salisbury was bloody magnificent.

And she had issued a challenge as surely as if she'd called him out.

It was to be a battle of wits, then, was it?

Something stirred and bloomed deep in his chest. He savored robust competition and, matching his sagacity against hers, appealed mightily.

Let's see precisely how miffed she is.

"Why don't you go below and wait for me there?" This time Pierce's gaze did include his sisters. "We can discuss matters when I join you. *After* I'm properly attired."

"Hmm, I don't think so." Bianca plopped her behind—not sank gracefully, but actually plopped hard enough to bounce *his* behind—onto the end of his bed. She toyed with the fringe edging her reticule.

She gazed around his chamber, inspecting each corner thoroughly before turning that enthralling tawny gaze upon him.

"So, Pierce, am I to live *here*? With *you*?"

5

Bianca's hackles rose at Lord Wainthorpe's censure, and she adjusted her position on the bed, giving her irritation time to ebb. She might've also wiggled a bit more exuberantly than necessary to increase his transparent-as-crystal uneasiness.

If she entertained a penchant for mischievousness, that is.

"Oh, this will never, never do. Miss Salisbury," Lady Timberly said, her voice tight with alarm. "You shouldn't be in a gentleman's bedchamber, and most assuredly, you cannot sit on his bed when he's within."

Up to this point, the Viscountess exemplified a

peeress's calm demeanor, but now she appeared rather flustered and clearly expected Bianca to bolt to the door straightaway.

Bianca arched an eyebrow and hid a grin when Pierce shifted his legs as far away from her as he could without wrapping them around his neck.

"You're here." She pointed out the obvious, knowing full well it was not the same at all.

"Yes," agreed Lady Mulbrury with a sweet smile. "But he's our brother. It's not quite so scandalous, you see."

"Still most indecorous," Popplewell grumbled. "Invading a gentleman's chamber. Him still abed."

"I agree wholeheartedly." Lord Wainthorpe looked pointedly toward the doorway. "If you please, ladies?"

A hint of disagreeableness underscored his request.

Eager to leave his comfortable bed now, was he?

If he wore a stitch beneath his banyan, Bianca would forfeit her virtue. Even with his hair tousled and stubble as black as soot covering his strong jaw, he managed to appear disturbingly attractive. He probably knew it too.

Heeding Lord Wainthorpe's hint, after collecting their gloves, his sisters filed to the doorway. They paused at the entrance and, as one, glanced at Bianca, clearly anticipating she would trundle below with them.

Intractable and pig-headed, Bertram had called her more than once.

Bianca had waited in the drawing room already. After nearly thirty minutes of pacing back and forth in the entirely too masculine room, its furniture severe and ruggedly masculine—*not unlike its owner*—she became impatient and plopped onto the couch.

Then her temper, the dratted mulish thing, poked its head up and started listing the offenses against her. The more she contemplated the situation, the more riled she became. Until she clobbered the cushion in her lap and jumped to her feet.

So, she'd explored her way to Lord Wainthorpe's chamber. His room hadn't been hard to find. The partially open door and feminine chatter, interrupted every now and again by his deep voice, lead her straight to his doorway with but one wrong turn.

Which brought her back to the present and the expectant faces regarding her.

"Do go along. I've much to discuss with your brother. Popplewell can act as chaperone." Bianca fluttered her fingers at Pierce's sisters and, hiding a less than dainty yawn behind her hand, swung her feet onto the bed and rested her back against the post.

Ah, much better.

Her leg was bothering her again today. Probably London's damp air.

Mrs. Garside laughed and looped her arm through Lady Timberly's. "Oh, I do like her, Nora. She reminds me of *me*."

At the nonplussed expression on Pierce's face, Bianca swallowed hard against the giggle bubbling up her throat. Clearly he hadn't a clue what to do with a female who didn't pour herself all over him.

Popplewell—poor fellow—looked on the verge of apoplexy, but the saucy maid grinned and exchanged a glance with Lady Mulbrury, who winked.

"Why don't you run along, Elsie?" Lady Timberly

suggested to the intrigued servant. "We'll be along shortly."

She gave Bianca a telling look.

Lady Timberly was not accustomed to being defied either.

Bianca never acted irresponsibly or rashly. Except with rebellion escalating in her veins and outrage hammering her heart, she'd tossed aside reasonable behavior.

"I'd just as soon hear what grand plans Lord Wainthorpe has for me now." She tilted her head, doing her utmost to read his bland expression.

His features gave nothing away. However, the silverish flecks around his irises gleamed a trifle brighter.

Annoyance?

"I'm sure you had something positively splendid in mind when you insisted Bertram assign you my guardianship," Bianca managed around another indelicate yawn. "I cannot wait to hear what it is."

"I'd rather like to know that myself." Lady

Mulbrury glanced at her sisters. "I'm sure we all would."

Bianca would eat tripe for a week if his lordship had any better luck than she in finding a satisfactory solution. Contriving a concerned mien, she plucked at the dark poppy-colored counterpane.

"You don't seem old enough to have a ward my age. Are you sure you're up to the task, Pierce? I'm not at all acquiescent."

Was that amusement warming the outer edges of his face?

How dare he be amused?

"I've been told I'm opinionated and stubborn. And I truly am a bluestocking and quite proud of it. No dowry either. Not a quid. Oh, and I have a limp." She joggled her sore leg. Only on occasion, but he needn't know that. "Makes me rather an undesirable, doesn't it?"

"No such thing, my dear," Lady Timberly assured her. "You're lovely. And some men actually appreciate a sharp mind and keen wit."

"I'm not certain that's ever been said of Pierce though, Nora," Mrs. Garside quipped, her voice quavering with laughter. "I believe other…*erm*…attributes are considered when he's gauging a woman's worth."

Bianca coughed to hide the embarrassed giggle she couldn't quite stifle.

A shadow darkened his lordship's angular features. Whether from Bianca's near insult or his sisters' chatter, she couldn't determine.

"I'm seven-and-twenty," he finally said, leveling his sisters a stern, be-quiet-now glower.

Only seven-and-twenty?

Really?

Bianca believed Pierce was somewhat older. Not terribly. In his early thirties, mayhap.

"And you are?" Didn't he know gentleman didn't inquire about a lady's age?

"Twenty on my birthday last month. Nearly on the shelf. In my dotage. Past the first blush of youth. Well on to becoming a spinster. A tabby, to be sure."

Though she jested, a thread of truth underscored her banter.

Mrs. Garside snickered rather indelicately, and Lady Mulbrury shook her head.

"Not in the least. I was nearly four-and-twenty when I married," she said.

Bianca cut a glance to the waiting ladies. They didn't dare leave her with their brother, but as long as the women were present, he couldn't rise.

Seems the Earl of Wainthorpe was in a fine pickle.

Actually, rather rapt expressions adorned his sisters' faces, too.

Tapping her chin, Bianca gave a slow nod. "I'll wager you're abed so late because you stayed up until the wee morning hours pondering an answer to our predicament, didn't you?"

She tipped her mouth into a jaunty smile, and he glared at her, only the jet of his pupils visible between his eyelids' slits.

Oh, provoking him was such fun though. Bianca couldn't resist another poke. "Is that why you're lounging about still?"

"No, Miss Salisbury. It is not," came his lordship's pithy retort. "I stayed up until the *wee* hours trying to discover where you flitted off to after I specifically said I wanted a word with you."

He didn't sound annoyed.

Not terribly, in any event.

A yawn forced its way to Bianca's lips, and she couldn't quite stifle the reflex. After puffing out an exaggerated sigh, she closed her eyes.

"Dear me, I'm quite fagged." She opened an eye slightly. "Don't suppose you would pass me one of those lovely, fluffy pillows you're leaning against?'

A laugh threatened to choke her as his eyebrows danced about his forehead in disbelief.

"No? I presumed as much. I'll wager their goose down too." Fatigue weighted Bianca's very bones, and closing her eye again, she fought the urge to lay on her side and yield to sleep.

"Oh, my Lord, she's just too precious," Mrs. Garside managed between chuckles.

Lady Mulbrury's mirth blended with hers. "Pierce, you're wearing the same obstinate expression you did as a child when you were forced to take your medicines."

Bianca opened her eyes.

An obstinate child too?

Not a surprise, really.

There he sat, arms folded across that wide chest with just a hint of crisp black hair peeking through the robe's parted collar. He met her gaze, and his coal-black eyebrows collided in a rather ominous scowl.

Did that thunderous look usually intimidate?

Bertram enjoyed blustering and scowling too, so she was quite accustomed to being glared at.

"Miss Salisbury—"

"Oh, pooh." She flapped her hand, hushing Pierce.

Pooh?

Had she really shushed the Earl of Wainthorpe?

Might as well do it up brown then.

"We needn't stand on formality, *Pierce.*"

His eyebrows contorted again, and if she wasn't

mistaken, a muscle ticked in his hard jaw.

"You may call me Bianca."

Head resting against the bedpost, she crossed her ankles. "I didn't sleep much last night either. But I'm afraid, no matter how hard I tried, I couldn't conceive of a respectable way out of our dilemma. Something to preserve my reputation against the gossipmongers who saw you win me last night. I don't want to even imagine what they are saying."

That was the absolute truth. She cringed just thinking of it. She would be labeled a slattern, and she knew too well the fate of such women.

Her humor evaporated. This wasn't a parlor game.

Popplewell spun around. He opened and closed his mouth thrice, his faded mustard-brown gaze swinging back and forth between her and Pierce. The black cloth patch covering one eye twitched with his agitation.

Bother.

Bianca had truly upset the valet. She sat straighter, acutely aware of Lord Wainthorpe's legs beneath the covers. In her determination to needle him, she failed to consider others' feelings.

How stupid and insensitive of her.

"*Respectable*?" Popplewell huffed, indignation rippling off his stooped form. "Your...*your* reputation?" he stuttered, his voice cracking with ire. "What about his lordship's reputation? Answer me that, will you, Miss? Did you give a single thought to what damage your childish actions would cause *him*?"

Remorse replaced Bianca's earlier frustration and irritation. She'd put them all in a difficult position. "Forgive me. I'll go below and wait there."

When did this get so turned about?

Now she felt guilty and ashamed. Both of which she swore as a child she would never feel again.

Shaking his head, Popplewell turned his back, then sliced a rabid glance over his shoulder.

"Why, unless his lordship marries you, I don't see how he can ever hope to regain his standing now," Popplewell snapped. "And you alone are to blame, Miss Salisbury."

~*~

"Now you're blathering utter nonsense, Popplewell. No one needs to marry anyone." Pierce seized his bedcoverings in one fist. Oddly irritated, he took control of the situation. "Ladies, I am rising, so either avert your gazes or prepare to be shocked."

Four women whirled away—Miss Salisbury the hastiest—and presented their backs just as Popplewell yanked one of the brocade drapes across the half of the window nearest the bed.

In one swift movement, Pierce rose then retied his banyan, making certain he modestly covered himself from his toes to his throat.

His sisters and Miss Salisbury remained motionless.

"Are you decent yet?" Rebecca half-turned her head but kept her gaze riveted on the mahogany wardrobe.

"I am." Perhaps not decent, but at least he was covered and felt more in command.

Head bowed, Miss Salisbury slipped off his bed, exposing shapely calves encased in peach-colored stockings in the process. Her stark black shoes didn't suit the ensemble.

They were her own, he would vow.

He glanced at her feet again. Rather large for a woman.

With effort, he subdued the grin that thought prompted.

She hustled to join his sisters, not once glancing in his direction.

Pierce bent a knee and scratched his head. "Miss Salisbury?"

"Yes?" She froze, her spine board straight and just as unyielding.

"I presume you stayed at the Timberlys' last night. Am I correct?" Lenora lived in the largest house. It only made sense. That information might also be used to their advantage to temper the gossipmongers' flapping tongues.

Bianca gave a short nod, exposing her fine nape

hairs. "Yes."

Good. Then her alibi was irrefutable. Only an imbécile wishing to be ostracized would ever infer that the Timberlys would be party to anything the remotest bit unsavory.

When he didn't say anything further, she scooted to his sisters' sides.

So daring and bold a few moments ago, and now the idea of glimpsing his nakedness had turned her into a timid mouse. Which meant, despite her earlier show of audacity, she led the sheltered life typical of a woman of gentle breeding.

The notion rather pleased, but Pierce mercilessly squashed the warm feeling.

She *might* be his ward, but he had no intention of forming an attachment. Still, he wanted to rub those rigid shoulders, caress the tension out of her neck, and assure her he would see to her best interests.

He hadn't the right to, of course. Not even as a proxy guardian.

To engage in such familiarity was unheard of unless

they were kin or affianced.

He almost snorted in self-disgust. Less than twelve hours after making Bianca's acquaintance and idiotic—*perilous*—thoughts were plaguing him. Time to put an end to the absurdity.

"I mean to shave, dress, and eat my breakfast before engaging in any sort of discussion."

After Pierce gulped down a pot of coffee laced with headache powders. He marched to the table containing the favored brew. His bloody skull threatened to split open every time he opened his mouth and with each jarring step. He poured a cup of coffee, ignoring Popplewell's affronted expression that his master should stoop to so menial a task.

"I shall call at Lenora's at ten." Cup in hand, Pierce glanced up. "No, make that eleven. That'll give me time to meet with my solicitor first. Will that suffice?"

"Yes, that will be fine." Lenora faced him and gave him a closed-mouth, apologetic smile. "I realize now I should've sent a note 'round rather than intrude upon you. Do forgive our impulsiveness. We were simply worried on your behalf and Miss Salisbury's."

Their intentions had been noble, even if their methods created a bigger hullabaloo.

Rebecca, too offered a contrite upward tilt of her mouth. "I fear we've added fat to the fire, haven't we, Percy?"

A barrel full, but nothing that couldn't be remedied. Pierce hoped.

Miss Salisbury drew her shoulders back and slowly pivoted. As she had done since last night, she met his gaze square on. She possessed admirable strength of character.

"You've all been discommoded enough on my behalf already. My lord, I've little doubt that the proceedings last night are not defendable in court, and even if they are, I don't want you as my guardian any more than you want me as your ward. I'll take my leave, and we can pretend this unfortunateness never occurred."

If only it was that simple. But the situation was not.

Pierce might be a scoundrel and *roué*, but he was

also a man of his word.

"It's not that simple, Miss Salisbury, but we'll discuss all that later. I have an idea. However, I want a bit more time to mull over the particulars before I share it with you."

He signaled to Popplewell. "See the ladies out. And send a note to Simmons, informing him I'll be at his office at half-past nine. If he cannot meet me then, he's to let me know what his earliest convenience is. Also send a missive to Churchgrove. I want him here within the hour."

Pierce crossed to his sisters, acutely aware of his bare toes kicking the hem of his robe, then gave them each a peck on the cheek.

"Thank you for caring enough to topple from your beds before dawn. I'm certain your husbands were none too pleased."

Their silence answered for them.

His brothers-in-law disapproved of him. More on point, they frowned upon his rakish lifestyle and his name being on chinwags' tongues or bandied about in the gossip rags.

Converted rogues, the lot, they felt it their duty to reform him as well. Just like Coventry, the overseer of the Wicked Earls' Club. Little did they know that most of the unsavory tattle they heard regarding Pierce was nothing more than a practiced ruse.

Still, he liked his faux risqué life. Enjoyed the freedoms it afforded him. Someday he was expected to marry and produce an heir. But not anytime soon.

In fact, perhaps never. Multiple relatives, three cousins to be precise, hoped to succeed him. In truth, a few kin quite begrudged him his inheritance. Those were the ones who resented his Indian blood and believed only an Englishman, through and through, ought to have been eligible for the entailments.

Evidently they knew little of their monarchy's lineage, none of which could claim pure English blood. Marriages to foreigners designed for political benefit shadowed sovereign after sovereign who'd sat upon the British throne.

Father went that route once. Did the dutiful,

expected thing. Married the blue-blooded English aristocrat his parents selected for him. Yes, he'd produced three daughters and a stillborn son from the union before his first wife died, but Father hadn't been happy.

He'd told Pierce as much.

Against his family's wishes, Father married for love the next time. When he died, he bore a peaceful smile, whispered *AamA's* name, and breathed his last.

Pierce didn't aspire to anything as precious. Still, a union with a woman of Bianca's ilk might prove quite entertaining. Satisfying even.

She most certainly piqued his interest.

"Don't look so distraught." Pierce took Bianca's hand and gave it a brief squeeze. At his sisters' skeptical expressions, he dropped it just as hastily. "I think you'll like my solution."

No joy or excitement sparkled in Miss Salisbury's eyes or tweaked her soft mouth upward. "Not unless it involves rewinding the clock so that this fiasco never occurred."

"I give you my word that your circumstances will be much improved, Miss Salisbury."

Those big eyes, wary and wounded, searched Pierce's face for a long, discomfiting moment before cynicism shuttered her vulnerability.

She snorted and poked him in the chest. "You expect me to believe the word of an infamous rakehell? Do you truly think me *that* daft?"

~*~

Pride still stinging from Bianca's frank retort, Pierce entered the Wicked Earls' Club just over an hour later on the off chance that the Earl of Coventry might be present this early in the day. Pierce couldn't claim surprise at her reluctance. If their positions were reversed, he would be less than enthusiastic too.

"I say, Wainthorpe, I didn't expect to see you this morning." Coventry extended his hand and accompanied Pierce into the sitting room. "Heard you provoked a bit of excitement while gaming last night."

"Pembroke or Benton felt duty-bound to share, no doubt."

"In point of fact, it was Sutcliffe." Coventry adjusted a bronze stag statuette on a side table. "He seemed quite concerned for you. Actually sought you out here."

"Indeed? He needn't have bothered." Sutcliffe was not a member. Just how did he know about the club? "Ever heard of Lord Fairfax?"

Coventry looked thoughtful for a moment. "Cannot say that I have."

"He's Bertram Normand." Pierce had never told another soul besides Coventry why he hated Normand so much.

"Bloody hell, you say. Well, I'm surprised you didn't run him through." He clapped Pierce's shoulder. "Great restraint on your part, I must say. Don't know if I'd have been as self-controlled. I take it you decided on another means of exacting your revenge for your mother's death?"

"I've ruined him. I own everything he has, and I've

bought all of his vowels. And, as you are no doubt already aware, I won his cousin too." Pierce's pulse quickened in anticipation. "Didn't even know he had a ward."

"Now that's an interesting complication." Coventry strode to the liquor cabinet. "Can I offer you a drink?"

"No, thank you." Pierce shook his head and flinched. "I'm still recovering from my over-indulgence last night. I've sworn off anything stiffer than claret."

"Coffee or tea, perhaps?" Coventry leaned a hip against the cabinet.

"Neither." Taking care not to shake his head again, Pierce eased himself onto an overstuffed chair. A man's chair. Not one of those dainty contraptions a man must perch on like an oversized canary—afraid to move lest he break the delicate thing.

"What brings you here at this hour, then?" Coventry had appointed himself the counselor and confidant of the earls who graced his club. Yet he also knew when to keep silent and not pry. Just as he wouldn't press Pierce any further about Bianca.

Forearms balanced on the chair, Pierce crossed his legs and twisted his mouth to the side. He was a hay cart short of a full load for even considering this.

"I'm off to my solicitor's." He pulled on an earlobe. "Miss Salisbury's mother's dead. Her father's whereabouts are unknown, and he, too, is presumed dead. And since that dunderhead Fairfax used her as collateral in a legal wager, I've decided to officially seek Miss Bianca Salisbury's guardianship."

By all that was holy, he was actually going to do it.

Become respectable. All for a wisp of a woman he'd just met.

"*You*? An innocent's guardian?" His countenance incredulous, Coventry burst into guffaws.

Pierce stiffened and uncrossed his legs. "It's not that bloody funny. Not humorous at all, actually."

"Yes, it bloody well is." Shoulders shaking, Coventry held his ribs. "Because you don't even realize the truth of it."

Pierce stood and withdrew the "W" from his lapel. He held it between his thumb and forefinger for a long moment, then laid it on a side table, the metal pinging against the polished wood. "I don't believe I have need of this any longer."

The unconditional acceptance amongst the earls was not something easily replaced or forsworn. Everyone, even irredeemable rapscallions, needed approval from those they respected and admired.

"Wainthorpe, wait." Coventry subdued his humor, concern replacing his amusement. "Don't be hasty. I meant no offense."

"I know, but if I am to gain Miss Salisbury's guardianship, I must dispense with all things disreputable."

Pierce shook his friend's hand.

"Goodbye, Coventry. And thank you."

6

As his landau turned down Berkeley Square, Pierce flicked his timepiece closed.

Nearly three-quarters of an hour late.

But for a good reason.

By chance or good fortune, Simmons had a meeting scheduled with another solicitor, this one familiar with Chancery Court proceedings.

Seems Pierce needed to file a petition straightaway and pad the complaint with a hefty bribe so that the case would be heard swiftly. He needed to prove but two things to bring a valid case before the court.

Was Bianca in peril—immediate or in the future— by remaining Fairfax's ward, and was Pierce willing to accept her guardianship?

A resounding *yes* to both questions.

A statement from Miss Salisbury expressing her concerns about remaining in Fairfax's custody and her reasons for wanting the guardianship reappointed might be considered helpful as well.

A trifling snag there.

She didn't necessarily want the custody transferred, didn't want to be anyone's ward, truth to tell. But once Pierce explained his plan, she was bound to come 'round.

Anyone other than Fairfax would be better.

Surely she would agree.

The unfortunate wager proved a much bigger obstacle.

Absolutely no mention should be made of the nature of how Pierce and Bianca first became acquainted. Even his difficult-to-startle solicitor's eyes had widened, and he'd blinked owlishly behind his spectacles when Pierce divulged that succulent tidbit.

Still, it was entirely possible the Lord Chancellor, a number of the common-law judges, or even a clerk might've heard of the ill-fated bet. If the court refused Pierce guardianship based on that fiasco, then he was prepared to ask Timberly to take on the role. In the meanwhile, Pierce intended to trundle Bianca off to Halverstone House until the matter was decided once and for all.

She would like Halverstone. The estate possessed pleasant gardens, and several walking paths meandered through the copses of trees and around a miniature lake. Very peaceful and inviting. Safe too.

The closest neighbors, Jules and Jemmah, the Duke and Duchess of Dandridge, were over a half-mile away. Bianca would get on well with the duchess, one of the few peeresses Pierce admired. Probably because her grace didn't affect pretentious airs. Their graces rarely journeyed to London, preferring the country's serenity to raise their growing brood.

If Fairfax pursued Bianca, he wasn't likely to find her sequestered at the seldom-used hunting lodge either. Why, Pierce hadn't visited the place himself in nearly five years. A skeleton staff managed the upkeep, so he would need to hire Bianca a lady's maid.

With a final lurch, the landau rumbled to a stop before Lenora's house. As Pierce stepped from the conveyance, he touched his beaver hat and gave a cordial nod to the passersby. Something he'd never done before, but he must make himself an agreeable chap for Bianca's sake. One never knew who might be on intimate terms with a stodgy fellow over at the Chancery Court.

"Ho, there, Wainthorpe."

Already at the risers, Pierce cut an impatient glance to the approaching gentleman. "Farley."

Owning the intelligence of a codfish, Farley was not high on Pierce's list of favored persons.

"Heard you won yourself a delectable piece last night." A gust of wind nearly wrenched Farley's top hat from his head, and he clapped a pudgy hand to the brim. "Sampled her yet?"

"Pardon?" Pierce stepped back onto the pavement, ire for Bianca welling behind his breastbone.

Never one to catch on quickly, Farley grinned wider and winked. "The red-head you won at cards last night. Heard she's a tempting armful. Everyone knows your appetite for women, so naturally, I assumed you bundled her straight to—"

Pierce jerked his hand up, palm out. "You may wish to stop there since if you continue and besmirch my ward's reputation with your vulgar insinuations, I'll consider it cause to call you out."

Farley's already pasty face paled further.

"I…I beg your pardon." Shaking his head, he backed up a pair of steps. "I swear I didn't know she was your ward."

He swallowed hard and retreated a few paces further, looking to his right and left as if seeking a place to sprint to.

"Must've misunderstood the whole affair, Wainthorpe. Serves me right for heeding the scandalmongers."

Pierce gave a sharp nod. "Indeed. Immediately upon the game ending, my sister, Lady Timberly, saw my ward to this very residence. I am just now calling upon them. You might want to spread *that* about."

Pierce resumed his climb but forced his lips upward and spared Farley a forgiving glance. "I'd be most grateful if you'd make the truth known at White's and Brooks's as well."

Farley's countenance brightened, and color flowed back into his features. He nodded eagerly. "I'd be happy to. Don't want people to form the wrong impression. You know how easily facts get misconstrued."

"Precisely."

Fifteen minutes later, a cup of heavily sugared oolong tea in hand, he lounged in Lenora's very feminine drawing room. She refused to serve coffee, more was the pity. Said it was un-British. She and Rebecca sat across from him on a jade silk brocade settee, and Amanda perched beside him on its twin.

To his consternation, Bianca had yet to make an appearance.

After his third polite sip of tea, he set his cup aside. "Is there a reason Miss Salisbury hasn't joined us yet?"

"I cannot imagine what the delay is, but I'm sure she shall be along shortly. She did mention a slight headache plagued her. I had powders sent to her room." Lenora rose and, after ringing the bell, paused at a side table and fussed with the floral arrangement. "May I ask what your solicitor advised?"

Pulling his earlobe, Pierce dragged his attention from the window again.

"I'd rather wait until Miss Salisbury is present so I don't have to repeat myself. But the gist is that if the Chancery Court can be persuaded that she's in jeopardy by remaining Fairfax's ward, my petition should garner serious consideration. I'm probably off my bloody head for even considering taking on the responsibility of the chit."

Amanda tutted. "No such thing. I think it very amicable of you."

Pierce gave Lenora a sheepish half-smile. "Though Simmons did warn," *rather bluntly*, "that my, ah, repute might factor unfavorably. He suggested it would be helpful if I were to have writs from several character witnesses."

At once, his sisters volunteered theirs and their

husbands' as well.

Although, those staid chaps mightn't be as eager as their wives to vouch for him. On the other hand, perhaps his brothers-in-law would think he'd finally come 'round to a respectable track and back him whole-heartedly. Several mutual acquaintances' names were bandied about as possible candidates who might lend Pierce support, too.

He could actually claim a few respectable friends himself as well.

Sutcliffe, of course. The Dukes of Pennington, Harcourt, Dandridge, and Manchester. Even Coventry might do in a pinch.

A queer, warmish twinge behind Pierce's ribs reminded him how fortunate he was to have such devoted sisters. Lest any of them confuse this singular genial act toward Miss Salisbury as a permanent change in his nature, he clapped his palms upon his knees.

"And if that doesn't suffice, I mean to impose upon you and Timberly, Lenora," Pierce said. "I know it will be a monumental inconvenience, and for that, I apologize. Surely the Chancery cannot object to your appointment. Far better you than I act as her guardian, should it come to that."

"I anticipated as much," Lenora said, standing back and perusing her handiwork. She tweaked a blossom. "I've already mentioned the issue to Mason, and he's in agreement. We cannot abandon the girl. He did ask a few questions, discreetly of course, about her background. Her parents were Ayra and Kevin Salisbury."

Pierce cocked a dubious brow.

Mayhap Timberly was not such a bad sort after all.

Pierce combed a hand through his hair and fought a yawn. Confound it, he was tired but even wearier of his hatred of Bertram Normand impacting his life.

"I swear," he said. "Not a single minute has passed that I haven't regretted ever setting eyes on Fairfax."

Making a sound of agreement in her throat, Lenora tilted another flower just so. "Have you considered what's to be done if the Chancery should rule against you? Perhaps even in favor of this Fairfax person?"

"I suppose I'll have no choice but to find someone to wed Bianca." *Out of the question.* "Or if that fails, marry her myself." *Not all that objectionable.* "But honestly, I don't foresee it coming to anything so drastic."

More's the pity.

Hadn't only a few hours passed since Pierce had resolved he mightn't ever wed?

Bianca truly had him at sixes and sevens, and worse, the notion of calling her wife didn't appall as much as it ought to. That reality was far more worrisome than his noble intent to become her guardian.

After some consideration, Rebecca selected a scone. Pulling it apart, she tilted her head and scrutinized him. "I must say, Percy, I've never known you to take such keen interest in someone else's welfare. Did I actually hear the words 'marry her myself' come from your mouth?"

"*Pshaw*," Amanda said, bestowing a doting smile upon him. "He's always been most considerate of those who hold his affections."

What the devil did she mean by that?

Surely not that he held Bianca in warm regard?

Did he?

Impossible on such a short acquaintance.

Hendricks entered before Pierce could put her straight. "You rang, my lady?"

"Yes. Please send a maid to check on Miss Salisbury." Lenora sat once more and took up the teapot to refill her cup. "Tell her Lord Wainthorpe awaits her."

Another ten minutes passed while his sisters plotted what flattering flummery they intended to include in their missives that would most likely sway the Chancery Court.

Pierce found himself staring at his cooling tea atop the table, the brew only a slightly lighter hue than Bianca's eyes. A mixture of excitement, anticipation, and dread made him tense. Uncertain even.

He couldn't explain it—didn't want to analyze why he was making such efforts on Bianca's behalf. Common decency, he assured himself. It was the right thing to do, he argued. Any person with any sense of integrity would do the same.

Ballocks, his altogether too forthright conscience, mocked.

Restless and eager to get on with it, Pierce shifted on the settee. Once again, he perused the drawing room entrance, then the music room's doors, and finally the scene beyond the window.

Legs cramping from sitting on the too-short settee and a headache yet pressing behind his eyes, Pierce stood, then wandered to the window.

He'd missed his morning ride through Hyde Park today.

He favored the outdoors, and now that he'd succeeded in Fairfax's ruination, he might actually consider a move to the countryside. Mayhap even Halverstone House.

His driver, Burroughs, stood at the head of the team, speaking gently to the horses.

People bustled hither and yon on either side of the rather busy, tree-lined street. The unseasonably pleasant, if somewhat breezy weather, brought

Londoners out in droves.

Pierce counted no fewer than nine nannies pushing buggies. An equal number of governesses were taking the air, their charges' hands firmly ensconced within theirs. Dozens of conveyances and riders crowded the cobbled street as well.

"Your pardon, my lady." The butler reentered on silent feet.

Pierce took one final glance down the lane before facing the servant. He halted halfway and swung back around whilst shoving the filmy panels aside.

By thunder!

He hadn't imagined it. That little minx.

Miss Salisbury, wearing that atrocious gown and an equally ghastly cape that looked to have been fashioned from a grain sack, hurried from the narrow track between Lenora's house and the neighboring manor.

She meant to sneak off, did she?

"Devil fly away with her!" Pierce bolted to the door, not even taking time to explain to his open-mouthed sisters what he was about.

Hendricks stepped neatly aside. "She turned right, my lord."

Pierce charged out the front entrance, pausing for an instant to locate his wayward ward.

With a sharp whistle and two bent fingers, he signaled Burroughs to follow. Before Pierce trotted down the last stair, the driver had gained the landau's seat. Determination in every step, Pierce lengthened his stride. His footsteps swiftly eating up the distance between them, he closed the gap between him and Bianca.

Shoulders slightly pulled forward and arms tucked to her sides, almost as if she were frightened, she trod onward. Her protective posture made Pierce want to wrap his arms around her and assure her he would keep her safe.

He was almost upon her now, and still she plowed forward, seemingly oblivious to the curious, occasionally rude, stares she garnered.

It was not just her ghastly attire.

A bearing surrounded her, a presence that

commanded attention. And her bright hair, unadorned by a bonnet, caught the sun's rays. Like precious metals, ribbons of burnished copper and dark gold-threaded the shiny tresses.

He glanced to his left. The landau rattled along just behind.

Good man, Burroughs. He was due an increase in wages.

Neck bent, Bianca strode purposefully onward.

Where to, Pierce couldn't imagine.

Surely not that rented hovel. Not only did the lodging house lay miles from here, but she would also have to pass through more than one seedy neighborhood to reach the establishment. Wearing her unfashionable attire, she risked being mistaken for a light-skirt and getting accosted.

Besides, last night he'd paid the holster to pack Bianca's belongings and send them to his residence. Something he forgot to mention when the women invaded his bedchamber this morning. After mentally inventorying her meager belongings, Pierce had made it clear that the landlord would incur his displeasure should as much as a hairpin be unaccounted for. Bianca's possessions had arrived shortly after she and his sisters had left.

A few more paces and Pierce caught up to her. Unaware of his presence, she marched resolutely forward, all the more reason she could not trundle to the unfashionable neighborhood unattended.

Should he shake her or embrace her for her foolishness?

Bianca's thoughts intruded upon one another as she rushed forward, her feet seemingly moving of their own accord. Her sore ankle protested the swift pace, but she pushed the discomfort to the back of her mind.

She must get away from the Timberlys' residence and that despicable man.

"I mean to impose upon you and Timberly," Lord Wainthorpe had said to his sister.

Of course he did. Heaven forbid that *he* actually take responsibility for his actions.

Yes, but if he hadn't accepted the wager, you'd still be at Bertram's mercy.

That truth galled her to no end.

From one unpleasant circumstance straight into another.

What was it Uncle Sylvester used to say?

From the frying pan into the fire?

He'd quote an adage for almost everything, and a twinge of loneliness encompassed Bianca.

She missed him. Unlike kind but aloof Aunt Florencia, Uncle had been warm and affectionate. Bianca didn't doubt he loved her, just like she knew Mum, with her sable hair and big, sad eyes had.

Bianca sighed and pulled her cape more snugly across her chest.

Never could she have imagined her one trip to Town would come to this.

Her greatest fear was upon her—possible ruination.

After taking the headache powders Lady Timberly sent up, Bianca had put aside her obstinacy and decided she should at least hear his lordship out.

Who knew?

He might actually have a satisfactory solution. Not

likely, to be sure, but what other options did she have at the moment?

Feeling slightly more optimistic, she'd re-pinned a stray strand of hair, pinched her pale cheeks, and straightened her spine.

But then she took a wrong turn and found herself in the music room rather than the drawing room. Unsure as to the propriety of using the entrance, she hesitated just behind the nearest open door.

"…the Chancery cannot object to your appointment," his lordship drawled. "Far better you than I act as her guardian, should it come to that."

Pressing her palm to her mouth, surely to keep from exposing her hiding place rather than from any emotional upset, Bianca remained rooted to the parquet floor.

"I swear, not a single minute has passed that I haven't regretted ever setting eyes on Fairfax." Such animosity weighted Lord Wainthorpe's words that she actually flinched.

Wainthorpe despised Bertram.

She knew it with absolute certainty. And if he hated Bertram, was it not possible that his lordship might also loathe her, Bertram's kin? Could there be more to Wainthorpe demanding her cousin assign him her guardianship?

The thought made Bianca physically ill and all the more determined to escape the earl.

Stupid ninny for thinking his lordship meant anything other than asking his sister to stand in his stead when he said he came up with a solution. Irrational to feel disappointed or hurt.

Or betrayed.

Exhaustion and worry must be affecting her emotions.

Desperate to put as much distance as possible between herself and Lord Wainthorpe, she had pelted to her chamber, changed her clothes, and fled the house. From this point onward, she would determine her own future.

Bianca's instinct to escape from where she was not wanted, where she would be a burden and a nuisance once again—and yes, her stubborn pride—urged her along. Glancing upward, she squinted at the street sign. It might as well have been written in Arabic, for it gave her no clue which way she should go.

She tried to ignore the few inquisitive stares her attire garnered from other pedestrians. For certain, she would need something more sensible to wear than this hideous ball gown. Not easily done when she had no idea where she was or how far away her let rooms were from here. Only that they were near Great Portland Street. For that matter, she didn't even know if she was headed in the right direction. But if she were to attain a respectable position, she must retrieve her meager wardrobe.

How many nights had Bertram paid for their lodgings in advance?

Would he be there?

If so, that complicated matters. A hidden pocket she'd sewed into her oldest gown contained a small stash of money. He would claim it his due for feeding and housing her.

The coins Bianca secreted away weren't enough to last long, but she must have those funds to survive. Angst gripped her, and her empty belly tightened further, reminding her she hadn't eaten since yesterday. And that meal was only bread, cheese, and an apple. Still, this wasn't the first time hunger had tormented her.

Thinking of agreeable things helped her forget the gnawing in her belly.

She mentally scrambled to conjure something pleasant.

Lord Wainthorpe's features intruded upon her contemplations.

A strong hand seized her elbow, and her heart vaulted to her throat.

Her other arm raised in defense, she swung around. The trembling organ in her chest didn't return to its proper place behind her ribs when that man turned out to be none other than a none-too-pleased Lord Wainthorpe.

Bother and blast. Ballocks, bunions, and boils, too!

A sound very much like a growl of frustration

gurgled in her throat.

She'd waited too long to sneak from the manor after hearing his deep masculine rumble disparaging his role as her guardian. Quite adamantly too. He'd foisted her off on the Timberlys in a manner as insensitive as if she were a raggedy, flea-ridden cat that followed him home.

Why bother pursuing her if she was such a nuisance, and he abhorred Bertram so much?

"Where do you think you're going? I am responsible for you, Bianca." His grasp on her arm remained firm, but his tone turned surprisingly patient. "Have you no care or consideration for my sisters either, after the benevolence they've shown you?"

Chagrin washed over her, heating her face, and she dropped her gaze to his polished-to-perfection Hessians.

Had her there, he did. His sisters had shown her nothing but kindness. Just because she was miffed at him for his bluntness and over-eagerness to be rid of her didn't mean she should forsake her manners or gratitude.

And why was she indignant in the first place?

Lord knew she didn't want Lord Wainthorpe as her guardian. Particularly if an ulterior reason motivated his request for her guardianship.

What type of fanciful plan did she think Lord Wainthorpe would contrive anyway?

Asking his sister to take on the guardianship made the most sense and was far more respectable than his doing so. And yet Bianca rebelled at the notion. Such fecklessness was rare for her, and she didn't care for the emotional flip-flopping one jot.

In the few hours since he sent her life tumbling into chaos, she'd lost her firm grip on her sensible temperament. Why he should cause such havoc irritated all the more. A chiseled jaw, smoldering eyes, and finely molded mouth had never turned her head before.

Mayhap because she'd never paid marked attention to men's jaws or eyes or mouths until she met him.

His lordship wouldn't learn about the lent rooms from her, however. If Bertram had paid rents until the end of the month as he had done in April, then she would have a place to stay for a short while. That ought to have occurred to Bianca before. But honestly, the wager and the hullabaloo that followed had so rattled her that she quite overlooked that important detail.

"Bianca?" Impatience tinged Lord Wainthorpe's voice now.

What believable excuse could she give? "I…"

A shiny black landau pulled up alongside them, and before she could finish her answer, Pierce neatly bundled her inside. Her waist throbbed where he'd encircled it to lift her inside.

He stood on the pavement, a forearm resting on the frame. "It's not safe or wise for you to gad about without an escort, my dear."

So it was 'my dear' now, was it? Like a doting uncle or indulgent older brother?

Or…a protector?

Never that. Never.

The earl didn't sound like a man who reviled her.

What game was he playing?

One Bianca didn't know the rules nor have the experience to win. This was dangerous ground, and she'd better tread most prudently.

A pair of matrons, necks craned and ears practically flapping as they strained to hear Bianca and Pierce's conversation, passed by at a pace a snail might exceed. The taller woman's mouth went slack, and she elbowed the other hard enough to make her wince and glower at her cohort.

"Octavia, doesn't she look just like that young woman Lady Clutterbuck was telling us about at the milliners? Remember, the redhead with loose morals?"

My hair is not red. It's chestnut brown.

Her companion lifted the pince-nez pinned to her redingote by a silver chain and balanced the eyeglasses on her thin nose. Lips puckered and eyes mere slits, she leaned forward, taking Bianca's measure.

"Sister, I believe you may be correct." Her focus switched to Pierce. "Do you suppose he's that scallywag her ladyship mentioned?"

Jolly good. More gossip.

"I was hardly gadding about, my lord," Bianca murmured so only Pierce could hear. "And we are drawing undesirable attention."

Affecting a pleasant expression she didn't at all feel, she slanted her gaze behind him.

A rough, disbelieving sound escaped him as he cast a glance over his shoulder. He dipped his head in greeting and flashed one of his charming smiles. "Beautiful day for a stroll, isn't it?"

So swiftly did the cronies dive to whisper in each other's ears, their poke bonnets smacked together, and the pair stumbled a few uneven steps.

Unbalanced, they tottered, and for a second, Bianca believed they might topple onto the pavement. Grabbing each other's forearms, they managed to steady themselves but speared blistering glares toward Pierce.

"Bianca, I need to give my driver instructions." He touched her arm, forcing her attention back to him. "I mustn't join you inside with those two tabbies watching."

Of course he mustn't. She was not a dimwit.

Her reputation already lay in tatters. She didn't need it shredded any further. Still, he might include her in his plotting. What did he plan to do now that he'd plopped her inside his landau?

His brows met, and he glanced at her feet. "I noticed you're limping."

Her ankle did throb a mite.

"I told you I had a limp." She lifted a shoulder an inch. "I suffered a broken ankle as a child, and the walk seems to have aggravated it."

"All the more reason for you to stay in here. Do you understand?" He gave the slightest jerk of his head toward the busybodies.

"I'm not a slowtop, Pierce. Of course, I understand."

Pierce shut the door, but Bianca quickly reopened it and poked her head out.

"Where is he—?" She stopped short when the women stopped and openly gawked. "Taking me," Bianca whispered to herself as she slowly eased the panel closed once more.

Just like that, she was supposed to comply?

Did anyone ever tell Pierce no?

Probably no women had, and against her will, she felt herself slipping under his spell as well. That rankled every bit—*more*—than his ordering her about as if he held the right already.

Sensible misses did not indulge in fluttering pulses and heated blushes when *roués* turned their attention upon them. Practical misses turned up their noses, presented their backs, and remembered their reputations above all else.

She flopped back onto the seat and folded her arms.

Oh, he made Bianca so deuced mad. And she generally possessed a cheerful mien.

Maybe she would slip out the other side. That would give him fits. Besides, how did she know that ridiculousness last night was even legal? He mightn't have any right to order her about. He'd soon find she was no meek, mousy miss.

She slid to the edge of the seat and peeked out the window.

There he stood, one hand on his lean hip and the other propped on the footrest. As if sensing her scrutiny, he angled toward her. Bending his sculpted mouth into a smile just this side of mocking, he shook his raven head and jabbed his finger, indicating she should sit back, out of sight.

Were all peers so commanding? Demanding? So cock-sure of themselves?

Hmph. Well, he would find she possessed a backbone and a mind of her own, as well as a tenacious streak not easily subdued.

She scooted to the other side.

Hound's teeth.

The ladies stopped at the corner and, under the shade of their fringed parasols, unabashedly scrutinized the vehicle.

Uttering a frustrated groan, Bianca collapsed into a corner.

Fine, she might not be able to slip away just now, but at the first opportunity, she would. A moment later, the equipage sprang forward, and she nearly lost her seat. She dared another glimpse out the window.

Pierce raised a hand in farewell before turning and striding in the other direction.

The chinwags' bonnets collided once more.

At least the eavesdropping matrons could vouch that Pierce hadn't boarded the landau. His thoughtfulness raised him minutely higher in Bianca's estimation. Wouldn't a notorious rake have taken advantage of the situation? Probably, but she'd heard Pierce was the epitome of discretion.

He presented quite an enigma.

A renowned rakehell but polite and considerate. A seasoned rogue up to his perfectly folded neckcloth—no, his iron black eyes—and yet, affectionate and attentive toward his sisters.

Who was the real Pierce Baxter Maximillian Chamberlain, the ninth Earl of Wainthorpe?

Lady Mulbrury had told Bianca Pierce's full name. She'd also told her he would only answer to Pritam, his Munda name, when he arrived in England.

How hard that must've been for him—an orphan and in a strange land. The new language and customs, and no parents to help buffer the confusion and fear. Bianca tilted her mouth into a grudging smile. He had adjusted well to his new life. Better than she would've done, for certain.

Bending forward, she attempted to memorize the passing landmarks. A sense of direction wasn't her strong suit, and after several minutes of the driver turning first one corner then another, she became thoroughly discombobulated.

Except…

As a familiar-looking house came into view, she wrinkled her forehead.

The Timberlys'?

Why the elaborate route then? The driver had made so many turns that her stomach and thoughts had become scrambled knots.

The carriage rattled into the mews behind the manor faster than Bianca thought safe, turned around so sharply that she was forced to brace herself against the side and ceiling to keep her bum upon the padded seat, then came to a rather jerky stop. Only her feet planted against the opposite seat prevented her from skidding onto the floor. Her empty stomach couldn't handle much more of this bouncing and careening.

An instant later, Pierce appeared out of nowhere and bounded inside.

The door hadn't even snapped closed before the conveyance was set into motion once more. She fought to keep her seat again. Perhaps the driver was new to his profession. He could do with a little—*a lot*—more practice.

Once certain she wouldn't be tossed onto the floor, she loosened her grip and demanded, "What in blue satin do you think you're doing?"

"Saving your reputation, my dear." Pierce grinned in devilment as he drew the shades, first on one side, then on the other.

How many times had he had his way with that roguish smile?

"By climbing in here and closing the shades?" Irony dripped from each word. "I don't believe that's quite how it's done, my lord."

He gave her another of his engaging grins, and her traitorous lips dared to tilt upward in answer.

"True, but no one knows I'm in here, except Burroughs, of course. And he would bite his tongue off before uttering a syllable to anyone. Even the trio."

"Trio?" Ah, he meant his sisters.

"Yes, those three precious, but interfering, female kin of mine." He jutted his thumb toward the back of the landau. "And I fear they've set their sights on you now too. Be warned, they aren't easily put off."

She'd learned the truth of that this morning. "They are probably peeved at me for sneaking away. I was unforgivably rude, wasn't I?"

"Not a bit of it. Rebecca applauded your daring. Amanda says I am to treat you kindly, or she will not permit her cook to make me any more of my favorite pink biscuits." Pierce waggled his brows and clasped his hands to his chest in mock theatrics. "A tragedy, to be sure. And when I left, after informing them I'd caught up to you, Lenora penned a letter—an advert for an abigail."

Warmth spread from behind Bianca's ribcage to her limbs. "They are truly lovely women."

"Indeed, and they recognize a woman of the same ilk." He gave her a lazy smile. "They'd have us wed in a thrice."

A jest? She wrenched her attention from the tiny bit of outdoors she could glimpse between the crack in the shade and the glass. Only sincerity played about the crooks of his mouth. Hunger couldn't account for her stomach's renewed frolicking.

Uncertain how to respond, she returned to perusing the narrow ribbon of landscape. The carriage rolled along, and unable to see what streets they passed, her dismay grew. She would never find her way to the lodging house now.

Nothing but a futile, rash idea from the start.

Pierce unfolded across from her, his legs stretched out and his fingers entwined across his flat stomach.

Bianca assessed the length of those impressive legs. A truly muscular physique. How could she have thought him soft and fleshy, with those angular cheeks and shoulders that strained the fabric of his perfectly fitted tailcoat?

A hot wave encompassed her as she recalled her audacity this morning.

Aunt Florencia had been slightly dotty and more than a bit eccentric. Especially when she nipped the sherry. Then she would ramble on about Mum—how Mum refused to come to live with them.

Because Mum still held hope Papa would return someday. He wouldn't be able to find her and Bianca if they moved from their humble room.

Perhaps the affliction was hereditary, and Bianca was slightly addled in the upper works too. She'd long suspected Mum was as well. Why else would she have stayed in London, pauper poor, when they could've lived comfortably at Elmswood with Uncle Sylvester and Aunt Florencia?

"Why are you here, my lord? Where are we going?"

No sense wasting time circling the pond, as Uncle Sylvester used to say. Direct and to the point prevented misunderstandings.

Pierce regarded her from beneath hooded eyes. "Because, Bianca, my dear, I mean to spirit you off to my hunting lodge until the Chancery Court either awards my brother-in-law or me your guardianship."

"But… But I heard you tell your sister you wished you'd never met my cousin. Which naturally means me as well. So why the pretense of wanting to be my guardian?" Tears blurred her eyes, and she dashed at her cheeks as a hot, sticky pair trailed over them.

Stupid, stupid girl.

"I assuredly do not regret meeting *you*, Bianca."

His voice held a warm note she didn't recognize but which rang with sincerity.

Tears flooded her eyes. *For pity's sake.* Bianca seldom cried and never for trivial reasons in front of others. Never. It wouldn't do for him to think she cared whether he still sought the appointment, and she swiped her face again.

Pierce made another one of those comforting noises in his throat, and then he was beside her, offering her his starched handkerchief. Which, of course, smelled deliciously masculine like him. Sandalwood, cedar, and perhaps a hint of cloves and peppermint too.

How was a girl to resist a man who smelled so wonderful?

Bertram always stank of sweat, garlic, and rancid cheese and Uncle Sylvester, of hair tonic and camphor.

Pierce's simple, tender act caused the dratted moisture to well even further, and though Bianca mentally ordered the waterworks to cease at once, more droplets spilled from her eyes.

"Such a time you've had of it, my sweet." Pierce wrapped one strong arm around her shoulders, cradling her to his side and pressing her head to his chest. "Have yourself a good cry. You deserve it, and I suspect you are long overdue. My sisters claim they feel ever so much better afterward."

And blast her for a fool, Bianca did cry, wetting the front of his jacket in the process. Several minutes passed with only the sounds of her weeping and his rhythmic breathing within the carriage as he held her. Finally, the well of misery ran dry, and her tears ceased.

Inhaling a raggedy breath, she shifted away from him and dabbed at her damp face. "Please forgive me. I'm not usually weepy."

Pierce pressed a bent knuckle to the corner of one of her eyes, catching a lingering crystalline droplet. "I think perhaps you have a stoic disposition, and you think crying a weakness that you seldom permit yourself to indulge in. But it's not a weakness, my pet. It shows you're caring and vulnerable."

Self-conscious at his tenderness following her lack of control, she gave him a wobbly smile. She was too deuced susceptible to him.

He cupped her jaw and traced his thumb across the seam of her lips.

A jolt surged outward from his gentle caress, and she was overcome with the most pressing need to turn her face into his palm. And kiss it.

Slowly, so gradually in fact, that Bianca was not aware Pierce had done so at first, he bent his head nearer to hers. He stopped his seductive onslaught on her mouth with his thumb, and an instant later, his warm lips brushed hers. The touch so brief—the slightest wisp but so tempting and delicious—yet alien desire tunneled through her every pore.

When he pressed into her harder, she didn't resist but opened her mouth to his tender nudges. But only for a few seconds before common sense shrieked for her to stop.

Bianca couldn't do this.

She was just another woman to Pierce.

And though she couldn't begin to understand what he might be becoming to her, the ugly truth was that afterward, he would go on his merry way, and she would be a woman ruined. Unfit for respectable employment, which left her with one option. To prostitute herself as many pathetic, desperate wretches had.

Even her own Mum.

That Bianca would not do.

She would not risk all for a practiced knave's scrumptious kisses. An immoral blackguard who had no right seducing his ward. She shoved away from him and delivered a stinging slap to his face before retreating into the farthest recess of the landau.

"I'm not, nor will I ever be, one of your strumpets, Pierce."

8

Pierce returned to his side of the carriage, and weighty silence descended in the vehicle. Not oppressive or angry. Melancholic, or perhaps disillusioned, better described the atmosphere. He seemed in the habit of disappointing Bianca, and that realization pricked something long-dormant buried deep in his chest.

As insane as it was, he wanted her approval. Why he should, when he didn't care a fig what most people thought of him, caused him concern.

She kept her head averted, and he traced her regal profile with his gaze. Likely, she was as deep in thought as he. Perhaps as muddled, too, given the shroud of awareness permeating the small enclosure.

Her hands lay primly in her lap, the oval nails short and neat. She wore no rings, no jewelry at all, for that matter. He would see her adorned in gems and the finest garments, though not because she required embellishments.

No, far from it. Beauty such as hers needed no enhancement.

It dawned on Pierce with startling amazement; he meant what he'd said to Lenora. He would marry Bianca, and not just if that was the singular way to keep her away from Bertram.

But only if she was willing, naturally. Despite his stained repute, Pierce was still considered quite a catch. Any fool holding a title was. She needn't tell him his earldom meant less than a nip of sugar to her, which made her all the more unusual and beguiling. He'd met her less than twenty-four hours ago, yet it seemed he'd known her for years.

What was it about this woman that penetrated his defenses? Had him actually considering matrimony?

Plowing ahead of yourself again there. First things

first. Wait and see what the Chancery Court rules.

That could—probably would—take weeks, and so Pierce had opted to quit London post haste. While Burroughs drove Bianca hither and yon earlier, to put the hounds off the scent, as it were, Pierce sent a note ahead directing Popplewell to pack his bags. He also requested that Elsie accompany them, for he meant to be on the road in less than an hour.

A tiny sigh escaped Bianca, and her shoulders slumped a mite before she squared them and continued to stare at the shade.

She truly did have an obstinate streak, the brave darling.

Pierce had made a colossal mistake, kissing her, though the kiss was the most delicious, the most moving he'd ever experienced.

She had every right to refuse his advances.

In fact, in some queer way, it brought him satisfaction.

Unable to resist the impulse, he touched his tongue to his lower lip. The sweetness of her plump lips yet remained upon it, and God help him, he wanted to sample the honeyed riches of her mouth again.

It would be worth another slap, but he was not a man who forced himself on women. He didn't relish being covered in bruises either. Bianca managed a surprisingly strong blow. If there ever were another kiss, she would initiate it.

And there would be another. And another.

He felt sure of it. But kissing only. Nothing more. He didn't deflower innocents. A wife, however…

Desire sparked between them, powerful and enticing, each time they were together, and unchecked passion simmered beneath her proper exterior. Odd thought, that he might find himself having to refuse her advances.

Another sort of challenge.

She would shrink in mortification if she suspected how easily he read her. Recognized the signs of willingness, even if she wasn't aware of them.

He touched a finger to his tender cheek, and the movement drew her focus.

She bit her lower lip, her repentant gaze trained on his face.

"I forgot to tell you, Bianca. Your possessions were delivered to my house this morning."

Relief brightened her eyes and softened her features. "Thank you, but how did you know where we lodged?"

"My man, Churchgrove, can find out almost anything with the aid of a coin or two slipped into a greedy palm."

A tiny, rather wry smile quirked her mouth. "I cannot imagine having that sort of power."

As his wife, she would.

For the third time in the same number of minutes, a similar thought intruded. Unwise, his thoughts rambling along that path. Instead, Pierce reflected on her honest observation.

He did take the privileges his title afforded for granted, and her furrowed forehead gave him pause. Had he become the very thing he detested? A self-centered elitist?

A taste, tangy and bitter, filled his mouth. It took a second to recognize it as disgust. He who'd judged so many was no better than they. What right did he, or anyone for that matter, have to condemn another?

What right did Pierce have to exact judgment on Fairfax?

The former captain had only been following orders.

AamA had aided the Munda rebels. Against Father's wishes and advice, too. Maybe if Father were at home when the raid occurred, he might've been able to intervene.

But AamA didn't deserve to die because of her involvement.

Fiend seize it.

Pierce's bloody conscience wouldn't shut up.

This temporary sojourn into respectability might be just the thing to escape the indulgent, self-absorbed life he had lived these past several years. Halverstone might be just the place to do so, too. He could ride all he wished, and if he recollected correctly, bass and trout populated the large pond while grouse and hares inhabited the fields.

Maybe he would become a gentleman farmer,

though what he knew of farming wouldn't fill a salt spoon. Also, upon arriving at Halverstone, he must attend to hiring additional servants straightaway.

He bent forward and lifted the shade an inch.

Nearly there.

From the corner of her eye, Bianca observed him.

Was she aware of his every move as he was of hers?

What was it about her that fascinated him so? Given her repeated peeks in his direction, she was equally enthralled.

The squab made a squishing noise as he settled against the plush backrest once more.

"Another couple of minutes and we'll arrive, Bianca. I'd like to depart within the hour."

"And how do you propose I enter the house without being seen?" Distinct frostiness tempered her question. "Perhaps your reputation is tarnished beyond repair, but I don't care to have mine equally as blackened. I do not have a fortune at my disposal nor a host of influential friends to rush to my defense when something untoward occurs."

Not ready to forgive him just yet, and why should she? He had acted the cur.

It was his duty to protect her honor.

"We are going to Rebecca's. Her residence is closest to mine." Pierce should've told her that from the onset. "You shall alight there, and I'll continue on to my house with no one the wiser. I'll collect my bags and your possessions, as well as Popplewell and Elsie. She shall act as your chaperone and abigail until Lenora finds someone suitable."

Bianca pressed her lips together, but she couldn't silence the protest simmering in her eyes.

What was it she was trying so hard not to say?

Ah, he should've considered. Women preferred picking their own lady's maid.

"Or if you would rather, you may conduct interviews for the position yourself. I could use your assistance hiring additional staff at Halverstone too." Pierce hooked his ankle across his knee, then tapped his fingers on his upper thigh. "If you would be so kind as to oblige me."

Fiddling with the clasp of her cape, she gave him a sideways look. "I've never had an abigail, and I do not require one."

"No," he said, straightening his cuff. "But you do require a chaperone, do you not?"

She conceded defeat with a small sigh. "You know I do."

Touché.

One point for me.

Pierce checked his pocket watch. "I shan't be above thirty minutes in returning. I must have your word that you won't try another stunt and dart away again. It would be most unfair to Rebecca."

Bianca, her chin tilted at what only could be described as a mutinous angle, regarded him with those thickly fringed amber eyes for a full minute before giving a reluctant nod. "I left to retrieve my belongings. And had I known you'd already collected them for me, I wouldn't have—"

Her voice trailed off, and she dropped her gaze to his boots.

He would forsake his carnal ways if that was the only reason she'd fled Lenora's, but Pierce let it go. Bianca had been through quite enough in the last eighteen or so hours.

"How far away is Halverstone?" She deftly changed the subject, but he was not daft enough to presume she had accepted her fate.

"A jot over five hours, but there are numerous inns along the way. We'll be stopping every ten miles or so to switch the team." He offered a compassionate smile. "I know this is most irregular, Bianca, and I'm sorry for it."

She laughed, a sad, fragmented sound that nicked his heart. A heart that hadn't felt much of anything in so long, he welcomed the faint sting.

"'Irregular,' my lord? You are a stranger, and you presume I want you dictating every aspect of my life? Do you have any idea how objectionable that is? And I have no choice, do I?" A derelict curl escaped its pin as she shook her head. "I should never have come to London. I just want to go home to Elmswood Parke."

"You can stay with Lenora, if you prefer." Even as he said the words, Pierce prayed Bianca would reject his offer. He wanted to get to know this intriguing woman with a temperament as wild as her bright hair.

"Oh, but I cannot," she refused, her eyes flaring with renewed ire. "You see, I shan't impose myself on another ever again."

Pierce arched a disbelieving brow and dropped his foot to the carriage floor. "Impose?"

"As a ten-year-old, I was thrust upon my aged aunt and uncle when my mother died from a stomach ailment. My father disappeared five years before that. Then when Uncle Sylvester died, Bertram inherited my guardianship. He made it perfectly clear I was an unwelcome obligation. And now, I've been foisted upon you. This," she waffled her hand between them, "was your doing, my lord, not mine. So you can suffer the inconvenience of my presence. Not the Timberlys."

No inconvenience, but a most lovely diversion. Mayhap more.

"But be warned, my lord." She stabbed her shabbily

gloved pointer finger at Pierce. "I am neither amiable nor biddable, and what's more, I don't want to be either. I predict a day shall soon come that you'll rue agreeing to my cousin's terms."

The carriage slowed, then rocked to a stop.

Try as he might, Pierce could only partially subdue his delighted grin, and even her castigating glare couldn't quell the upward twitch of his mouth.

"That sounds very much like a challenge, Bianca. And I whole-heartedly accept."

He placed a finger across his lips, contemplating her. "I also have a prediction."

"I'll just bet you do," she muttered, trying to squeeze farther into the corner.

Where was the bravado of a second ago?

"I predict a day shall soon come," he said, "that you'll beg for my kisses."

~*~

Bianca nearly vaulted off the seat.

Of all the insufferable, arrogant balderdash.

Beg for the handsome lout's kisses, indeed.

We shall see.

Summoning her most dazzling smile, she stood and partially stooped over Pierce—all casual masculinity splayed against his seat. She drew her fingertip from the red hand mark on his face to the corner of his mouth.

His pupils dilated, and his breath quickened

Fascinating.

Was that what happened to a man when aroused?

Did it hold true for a woman too?

She dipped lower still, and his mouth parted the merest bit as he cupped her sides with both hands.

He flexed his fingers, digging the tips into her ribs.

So wicked of her. But the power proved heady and unlike anything she'd ever felt before.

Inch by inch, she bent her neck lower and lower still until only a finger's distance remained between her mouth and his. Instinct made her run the tip of her tongue across her bottom lip.

His heavy lids drooped over those penetrating,

mesmerizing eyes—*thank God, for I was about to lose myself in those fathomless depths*—and he released a shuddery breath.

"What do I get if you lose, Pierce?" she whispered in the sultriest voice she could muster.

"I shan't."

At the seductive timbre of his voice, she swallowed hard. He ran his hands up and down her sides, and only by biting the inside of her mouth did she keep from gasping at the intoxicating sensation.

"In fact, I'll up the stakes, my sweet. You'll plead for much more than my kisses, Bianca."

She bit the inside of her cheek to keep from gasping.

Playing unfair, was he?

Well, she could too.

"*Tsk.* Is that any way to speak to your new ward?" Resting one hand on his thigh, she tapped his mouth with her finger.

He pursed his lips against the fingertip.

Such burning heat vibrated up Bianca's arms that it

was all she could do not to snatch her hand away. A startled puff of air did escape her this time.

She was dabbling in hazardous territory. One that he had far more expertise in than she. No doubt his vast experience led him to believe he knew how she would respond.

Fine then, she would be completely unpredictable.

Go port when he assumed she would go starboard.

Giving him what she hoped was a siren's smile—after all, she had no practice at this seduction business—she said, "I'll shall be permitted to stay at Elmswood Parke if, over the next month, I do not willingly kiss you. And you must agree to let me live there. Oh, and no plying me with your seductive wiles either."

"We shall see." A lazy chuckle rumbled from Pierce's broad chest, and he pulled her between his powerful legs. "And what do I get if you lose, my sweet?"

He nuzzled the hollow where her neck met her ear—*oh, sweet mother of God*—and her dratted knees turned to gruel.

The latch rattled, and she jerked away mere seconds before the door swung open.

Scandal averted.

By a hair's breadth.

As Burroughs helped her descend, Bianca's heart yet banged against the hollow of her throat. Thank goodness for her cape's high clasp, which hid her hopscotching pulse and the clear evidence of her transgression. And desire.

She faced the landau and gazed up at Pierce.

Unperturbed, his mouth curved the merest bit; he appeared inordinately pleased.

"You asked what you shall receive if I lose. Nothing, my lord. Absolutely nothing. For if you succeed, I shall have already forfeited all that matters to me." A tremulous smile bent her mouth. "My virtue, my reputation, my pride, and any chance for a respectable future."

9

Halverstone House

Shire County, England

Deep night shrouded the countryside by the time Burroughs tooled the coach to Halverstone House's front steps. Pierce yawned and brushed his fingers across Bianca's satiny cheek.

"My sweet, we are here."

The coach that had carried Popplewell, Elsie, and everyone's luggage stood a few feet farther along the drive.

Bianca stirred, then slowly opened her eyes, blinking groggily. Her head lay against the curve of

Pierce's shoulder, the arm cradling her to his side, having fallen asleep some time ago. Yet he hadn't been able to bring himself to shift her away and bring relief to the numb appendage.

Covering her mouth, Bianca yawned daintily and straightened. She frowned, an endearing furrow of confusion. "How did I get beside you? I distinctly remember sitting over there when we boarded the coach after our last stop."

She pointed to the opposite seat.

He gave her an unrepentant grin. "You were bobbing about on the seat like a fledgling robin clinging to a frail branch. I feared you'd tumble to the floor and perhaps injure yourself."

"Oh. Then thank you for your consideration." She scooted across the vehicle and collected her reticule and a tattered hatbox.

No false dramatics or pretense of offense.

No, his ward was a sensible miss, and perhaps they might strike a truce while they were here. He'd like that more than he cared to admit—even to himself. In fact, he looked forward to their stay at Halverstone more than he'd anticipated anything pleasurable in a great while.

The door swung open, and a haggard Burroughs lowered the step.

"Burroughs, you have earned an increase in wages. How does twenty—no-thirty percent sound?"

Sudden vigor brightened the driver's lined eyes.

"That's very generous of you, sir."

"No more than you deserve." Pierce exited first, nodding to the assembled staff as he handed Bianca down.

Digby, the butler, stood on one side of the stone stairs with his wife, Halverstone's housekeeper and cook. Two maids of all work, as well as the groundskeeper—Broomfield—stood on the other side. Each appeared as if they'd piled out of bed mere moments before.

Probably had when the first conveyance arrived.

"I trust the journey wasn't overly rigorous, my lord?" Digby nodded a welcome, several stubborn strands of hair poking straight upward at the back of his head, making him look like a disgruntled Asian flycatcher. His inquiring gaze strayed to Bianca for a second.

"Not at all. We frequently stopped, hence our late arrival. I apologize for not sending word ahead." Pierce drew Bianca forward. "May I present my ward, Miss Bianca Salisbury?"

To their credit, except for a twitching brow or two, his staff remained remarkably composed at his declaration.

After making the obligatory introductions, Pierce motioned to Broomsfield. "Please help Burroughs with the team, then seek your bed."

"Aye, sir." Hitching his mouth into a grateful, sideways smile, Broomsfield toddled toward the waiting team.

Assessing Bianca with an acute glance, Mrs. Digby stepped forward.

"My lord, as we were unaware you were coming, I fear only the lord's and lady's chambers are prepared." She sent the maids an apologetic look. "I can have another chambered readied, but it will take an hour or two."

It was well past midnight already, and Bianca could

barely keep her eyes open. The maids exchanged bleary gazes, and one yawned behind her hand.

"Miss Salisbury can use the prepared chamber for tonight and move to another tomorrow." Pierce intended to prove his agreeableness to his ward straight off. "Is that acceptable to you, Bianca?"

Bianca threw him a disconcerted look.

"Why, yes. I should hate to be an imposition." She offered Mrs. Digby a cautious smile. "I can ready the other chamber myself tomorrow. No one need wait upon me. I'm used to fending for myself."

"*Tut*. No need for that. You are a guest and will be treated as such." Mrs. Digby signaled the maids. "Be off with you. I expect the fires lit by half-past five as usual."

"Yes'm," they chorused before bobbing shallow curtsies and scampering back inside the manor.

A few minutes later, Pierce stood just inside the lady of the house's chamber. He'd never actually been within its walls before, and he scrutinized the pretty, feminine room with a critical eye. Finding nothing amiss other than the coverlet and draperies clashed with Bianca's bright hair, he gave her a weary, closed-mouth smile.

Hound's teeth, he was tired.

"I trust you'll be comfortable here, Bianca. Should you need anything, the bell pull is just to the right of the fireplace." Pierce indicated the rose and gold tasseled cord.

Bianca nodded a bit distractedly, her focus on the door between her chamber and Pierce's.

"Mrs. Digby? Might I trouble you to lock the connecting door and take the key with you to prevent any speculation about untoward behavior?"

Pierce cursed silently. He ought to have thought of that too. No wonder Bianca had looked so taken aback when he'd suggested she use this bedchamber.

"But of course." Mrs. Digby beamed her approval and hurried to do as bid. "What a lovely, upright young lady your *ward* is, my lord."

Mrs. Digby emphasized the word ward, making it clear she would permit no skullduggery beneath Halverstone's corbelled vaulted roofs. Pierce might own the building, but Mrs. Digby controlled the goings-on within its four-story stone walls.

Once the door had been locked, the handle tested thrice—*just to be sure*—and the key attached to the chatelaine at Mrs. Digby's waist, the housekeeper waited at the door. She clearly wasn't budging until Pierce quit the room as well.

"Tomorrow, I'll give you a tour of Halverstone. Goodnight, Bianca." Fatigued to his marrow, Pierce stifled a yawn.

In the process of removing her bonnet, Bianca paused. She seemed quite lost, poor thing. "Goodnight, my lord. Mrs. Digby."

Good of her to include the housekeeper. Bianca had found an ally there already.

Pierce closed the door and was brought up short by Mrs. Digby, arms akimbo and mouth pursed, blocking his path.

"I'm not going to ask how that young woman came to be your ward, my lord." She slid her attention to the carved door behind him for an instant. "But even I can see she's an innocent with a good heart, and I'll not have any shenanigans under my watch."

"I assure you, nothing disreputable will occur. We are only here to keep Miss Salisbury safe from her former guardian." Pierce half-held his breath lest God smite him for the brazen lie. Yes, he wanted to keep Bianca safe, and yes, he found her enticing, but something far more powerful and compelling about her had awakened his interest.

"*Hmph.* Well, I do hope you know what you're doing." After leveling him a starchy stare, Mrs. Digby's features softened. "I'm to bed, my lord. Unless you need something else?"

"No. No. You've lost enough sleep already." Exhaustion weighting his very bones, Pierce entered his bedchamber to find Popplewell puttering about. "I'll undress myself. You've had a long day too. Seek your bed."

Popplewell sniffed in disapproval but proceeded to the doorway nonetheless.

"Very well, my lord. I hope you don't intend to make a habit of this, however."

"Never fear. Your position is secure," Pierce

assured him while untying his neckcloth.

"You have a visitor. I tried to move *it*, but *it* hissed and swatted at me." The valet pointed a knobby finger at the bed upon which lay a contented calico cat. With a stiff nod, Popplewell departed.

And left the feline behind.

His way of wreaking revenge, no doubt.

Once stripped, Pierce swiftly cleansed his teeth, then fell into bed. The cat gave an annoyed yowl, but rather than jump to the floor, she glared at him with one green eye and one blue before prancing to the foot of the bed and making herself comfortable once more.

Pierce was simply too tired to care. Releasing a half-sigh, half-groan, he closed his eyelids. A pair of solemn, cinnamon-colored eyes floated across his mind before sleep claimed him.

Sometime later, a muffled cry roused Pierce from his slumber. He raised his head, angling his ear toward the attached chamber.

Had Bianca cried out in her sleep?

Another distressed sound echoed through the wall

separating their headboards.

Was someone in her room?

Fairfax?

His blood congealed in his veins.

Pierce tossed the bedcoverings aside and, as his feet met the carpet, snatched his banyan from the end of the bed. After quickly tying it at the waist, he drew open the bedside table's drawer and blindly searched about for the key he prayed was still there. Gripping the cold metal in his palm, with long, swift strides, he crossed to the adjoining door.

Taking care to turn the lock as soundlessly as possible, he slipped the key into his silk robe's pocket and toed open the door. A thread of moonlight filtered through a crack in the window coverings. He searched the room for an intruder and, finding no one, released his breath.

Bianca still thrashed about in her bed, whimpering.

"Shh, my sweet," he whispered.

She'd be livid to know he possessed a key and that he'd dared to enter her bedchamber without permission.

But he couldn't ignore her suffering. Treading carefully in the dark chamber, lest he bump into furniture and stub a toe or awaken her, he crept toward her bed.

What tormented her so?

Bending over, he touched her shoulder with two fingertips.

"You're safe, Bianca. I'm right next door, and I promise no harm will come to you."

She sighed, turned onto her side, and tucked one hand beneath her cheek. Her hair splayed out across the pillow. Why wasn't he surprised she didn't plait the mass at night? Or had she simply been too tired to fuss with a braid before retiring?

He caressed her cheek.

One kiss. That was all he wanted. One to reassure and comfort her.

Even as he dipped lower, his conscience chastised him.

Fiend. Opportunist.

"You needn't fear any longer, my pet. You are mine to protect now." Grazing his mouth over her soft lips,

Pierce breathed in her scent, and she sighed again, snuggling deeper beneath the bedclothes.

Reluctant to leave and unsure why, he stood beside her bed for several minutes more. Somewhere in the house, a clock chimed three of the clock.

So much for getting a good night's sleep.

Just to be certain no one could enter her chamber uninvited, he checked the window latches and the lock to the balcony door. Finding it unsecured, he slid the bolt home. The scraping echoed loudly in the now silent chamber.

Yawning, and with one last look at Bianca, he shook his head. Winning that minx had set his life on a new course. A path he suspected he had little control over.

~*~

Six days later, Bianca rested her forearms on the balustrade of the balcony and took another bite of strawberry preserve covered toast.

Unaware that she was observing him overhead, Pierce, attired only in a shirt and black pantaloons, practiced his fencing moves on the flagstone terrace below.

His boots clacked and clicked as he lunged and thrust, his sweat-dampened ebony hair clinging to his temples and forehead. That tempting thatch of black hair at the vee of his collar appeared every now and again as he twisted and turned.

She felt quite the voyeur as she spied upon him each morn.

Perhaps she made a noise or her shadow alerted him, but he suddenly glanced upward, and her stomach tumbled over itself.

Caught at last. A wonder he hadn't discovered her sooner, truth to tell.

A knowing grin tipped his mouth as he bent into a courtier's exaggerated bow.

"Good morrow, my fair lady," he called up. "How did you sleep? Have you broken your fast?"

"I slept well, thank you, and I just breakfasted here

on the balcony. It has such a lovely view of the grounds."

And their owner, too.

Perusing the landscape, she brushed the crumbs from her hands. Once she'd slept in the adjoining chamber and unpacked her scant belongings, there didn't seem any point in moving to one of the other rooms and causing the servants more work. Besides, this quaint balcony overlooked a charming gazebo and a large pond. Bianca enjoyed eating breakfast, reading, or taking tea here.

Pierce wiped the perspiration from his forehead with the back of his hand. "Will you honor me with a walk again today?"

"That would be lovely. What time?"

"In thirty minutes?"

"I'll meet you on the terrace." They'd fallen into a routine of taking a stroll together before noon each day and playing a game of chess or reading in the library in the afternoon. She leaned far over the rail and called to him just before he entered his study directly below her room. "I expect you to allow me a rematch today. I nearly won yesterday."

"I can deny you nothing, my sweet. A rematch it is."

Pierce gave her a saucy salute and disappeared inside.

She sighed and stood upright. He had acted the most charming of hosts, and her resolve to resist him spiraled lower and lower. Why did he have to be such a rapscallion? If he weren't, if he offered her respectability…

But he hadn't.

~*~

That afternoon, sitting across from him, Bianca pressed her forefinger to her lips and narrowed her eyes in concentration as she studied the chess pieces. Unlike Uncle Sylvester's set, this expensive chess set was of French origin. She'd claimed the yellowed ivory pieces while Pierce played with the red.

"I am going to win today, Pierce."

"Perhaps. You're a worthy opponent. Your uncle taught you well." He exuded relaxed masculine confidence, drat him.

"We played often," she said, still studying the board. "Did your father teach you the game?"

"Actually, Lenora did. She also taught me to fence."

That gave Bianca pause, and she shot him a surprised glance. "She did? Somehow, I cannot see Lady Timberly wielding a foil."

A low chuckle rumbled forth, and he winked as Miss Millie, the pregnant tabby, rubbed against his calf. "Well, she might've hired the master who instructed me."

"You did that just to break my concentration, you bounder." Bianca shook her finger at him. "It won't do you any good—"

The cat leaped onto the chessboard, scattering the pieces hither and yon.

Pierce let out a guffaw and scooped Miss Millie

into his arms, hugging her to his chest and dropping a kiss atop her head. "That's my girl. You saved me from a humiliating defeat."

Bianca pursed her lips and flopped back into her chair. "I swear she did that on purpose, the jealous vixen."

"Has she reason to be jealous?" Sincerity replaced his hilarity, and he tilted his head, his dark-eyed gaze probing.

Caught off guard, more by the sudden rush of emotion his question caused than the inquiry itself, Bianca shrugged, then stood.

"As if I'd be gullible enough to admit such a thing to you." She bent and gathered the pieces nearest her. "Besides, who is envious of a tubby, ragged-eared cat? Certainly not I."

He lowered his mouth to Miss Millie's ear. "Methinks the beautiful lady has a valid point. I also think I should help pick up the mess *you* made."

In a thrice he kneeled beside Bianca and helped collect the ivories. They reached for the last piece at the same time and bumped heads.

"Ouch," Pierce grunted and sat back onto his heels.

"Ow," she yelped, slapping a hand to her head. Her focus dropped to his coat. "Your jacket is covered in cat hair. Popplewell will have an apoplexy." She dropped to her knees before him. "Hold still so I can remove the worst."

She bent her neck to avoid those penetrating eyes and brushed at Pierce's shoulders and chest. Stupid thing to have volunteered to do, for touching him caused all manner of other sensations to reverberate through her.

To his credit, Pierce held stock still, hands at his sides. Despite his promise that they would share more kisses, he'd acted the perfect gentleman this far. Attentive and polite, the model of decorum, he'd ensured her every need was met while never straying into taboo territory with as much as a suggestive look.

Nonetheless, the room fairly crackled with sensual electricity. At least she thought so. Given his immense experience, he mightn't be as aware.

As she picked hair after hair off his coat, she wished she wasn't so conscious of him breathing into her scalp. Of late, her body had become a foreign entity. Peculiar sensations and yearnings she could neither identify nor had the scarcest notion of what to do about assailed her.

This close, his cologne enveloped her, and Bianca admitted to herself she was envious of the cat. For the wanton thing made no pretense about her affection for Pierce, and he readily caressed the demanding feline.

Still, Bianca was determined not to fall prey to his practiced ways and redoubled her efforts to be immune to him. So what if he smelled splendid, possessed chiseled cheekbones, and had a muscular chest?

Her growing fascination was at best imprudent, she scolded silently. A flush of awareness heating her cheeks, Bianca finally sat back. "I fear that's the best I can do. The hairs cling to your coat."

Pierce cleared his throat, then cupped her shoulders. "Bianca, I—"

"Sir, there are two gentlemen to see you. They claim you hired them in London." Digby didn't as much as bat an eye upon finding his employer and his ward kneeling on the floor together.

"Thank you, Digby. I shall see them in here." Pierce stood then extended his hand to help Bianca up.

She would rather not touch him again. She didn't trust her reaction, but she couldn't very well lumber to her feet with the butler looking on. Placing her fingertips as lightly as she could in Pierce's palm, she allowed him to assist her.

"Shall we play again tomorrow?" He smiled, his white teeth a startling contrast against his olive skin. "I'll make sure Miss Millie does not interrupt us this time."

Bianca should say no. No good could come of her budding feelings. But she nodded nonetheless.

She wasn't any different from her mother after all, was she?

10

ierce snipped a final rose stem and placed it in the basket dangling from his arm. Satisfied with the two-dozen blossoms he'd cut, he dropped the clippers inside the basket as well.

Whistling, he headed for the house. Another amiable week had passed, and he quite liked the domestic routine he and Bianca had fallen into. He appreciated the peace and slower pace of country life, too. Most especially, he enjoyed Bianca's witty company.

He lifted the basket and sniffed the roses.

These were for her.

What a sentimental sot he'd become. Almost daily,

he found an excuse to give her something. A feather, an agate, a special volume from the library, a ribbon for her hair, or quite often as he did today, blooms from the gardens.

She adored flowers, and he cherished the radiant smile that lit her eyes with joy when he presented another bundle to her. He suspected he could hand her a fistful of weeds, and she'd respond with the same enthusiasm.

As he strode toward the house, he examined the balcony she so favored. The balcony from which she'd spied upon him each morning that first week. Now, she simply situated her chair next to the balustrade and watched her fill.

Three days ago, he'd nearly strained his groin showing off for her.

A few minutes later, he found Bianca in the drawing room. Actually, her singing led him to her. Halverstone often rang with her clear alto voice. A voice Pierce had come to cherish, whether she was speaking to him, laughing at Miss Millie's antics, or crying out in her sleep as she continued to do on occasion.

When he entered, she glanced up from the flowers she was picking the spent blossoms from, and her face broke into a winsome smile.

"*More* flowers, Pierce?" She pointedly looked at three other vases filled with cuttings from the gardens.

"Yes. It gives me pleasure to give them to you."

She accepted the basket and, after setting it on the marble-topped table, lifted a pink rose with yellow edges to her nose. "They smell divine, don't they?"

"They do." He rested a hip against another table and crossed his arms. "Can you leave that and the fresh flowers for a servant? I have a surprise for you."

Setting the rose down, Bianca shook her head. She'd done something different with her hair, and the new style became her.

"You really mustn't keep spoiling me, Pierce. It gives the wrong impression. I'm sure the servants think there's more between us than a mere guardianship."

She considered a gift of flowers from his garden spoiling her?

And no one had better dare infer anything improper between them. He'd taken utmost care that their interactions were above even stringent Mrs. Digby's reproach.

"Come." He held out his hand. "The flowers can wait, but I cannot."

"All right." She hesitated for only a second before slipping her hand inside his and allowing him to lead her to the entrance.

In the corridor, he released her hand but took her elbow instead. He glanced at her feet. Good. She wore her sturdy black shoes, perfectly suitable for a short trek to the stables.

"Where are we going?" She smiled up at him. "I confess, you've roused my curiosity."

He'd like to rouse much more than that, but he'd sworn to himself to amend his roguish ways as far as Bianca was concerned.

Pierce tweaked her nose, then quickly scanned the passageway to make sure no one had witnessed him. He'd taken two liberties in as many minutes after he'd vowed to himself to be the model of decorum around her.

"I'm not telling you, Bianca. It wouldn't be a

surprise then, would it?"

Pierce steered her in the stable's direction. When they entered, the pleasant aromas of fresh hay, horseflesh, and feed surrounded them. He took a moment to inhale, savoring the familiar, soothing smells.

Bianca didn't press him about her surprise. Instead she smiled at Broomsfield as he approached, carrying a sliced apple.

Broomsfield ducked his head deferentially. "Sir. Miss."

"I'll take those." Pierce took the pieces of fruit. "This way, Bianca."

He directed her to a far stall. As they neared, a creamy, blue-eyed horse's head appeared over the top of the gate.

"She's yours, Bianca."

Bianca gasped and turned to gape at him in wide-eyed wonderment. "Oh, she's quite the loveliest horse I've ever seen. And she has blue eyes."

"Luna is a four-year-old Cremello. Very gentle, but according to Dandridge, whose arm I had to twist mightily before he sold her to me, she's very intelligent, too. She's been trained to a sidesaddle and English saddle."

Bianca tentatively approached the animal, then glanced over her shoulder. "I haven't ridden in years. I may be a bit out of practice."

"Well, then, I guess I'll have to include daily rides in my guardianship duties." The chore didn't seem half as troublesome as it would have a couple of weeks ago.

The horse extended her neck and sniffed.

Careful to keep from staring the mare in the eye and alarming her, Bianca lifted her hand and let Luna sniff the back. "I do appreciate your thoughtfulness, and I shall ride her while I'm here. However, I cannot take her with me when I leave."

"Why must you leave?" Pierce offered Luna an apple slice, which she greedily accepted and chomped contentedly. "Aren't you happy here?"

"Yes." Bianca didn't look at him but continued to pet Luna while making crooning noises.

"Bianca? You don't have to leave."

Sighing, she dropped her hand to her side and faced

him, her expression guarded now. "We have an arrangement. An agreement. I'm leaving in a few days."

"Agreements can be amended." Pierce patted Luna's wither before wiping his sticky fingers on a cloth hanging from a nearby peg.

"Not this one. I have too much at stake. I've set a course, and nothing will deter me from it." With that pronouncement, Bianca lifted her skirt and took her leave.

"That's what I thought until I met you, my sweet," Pierce muttered after her retreating form.

~*~

A bump against her hip roused Bianca from a delicious dream in which Pierce kissed her as she slept. The grazing of his lips against hers seemed so real that she touched her fingertips to her mouth. Another nudge followed by the sounds of a cat grooming itself revealed Miss Millie had made herself comfortable on Bianca's bed.

Again.

"You're becoming far too accustomed to my coverlet, Miss Millie," Bianca mumbled against the pillow cradling her cheek.

The calico had found her way into the bedchamber once more. Several times since Bianca arrived almost three weeks ago, the determined feline managed to sneak onto her mattress sometime before dawn.

For the past week, since rebuffing Pierce in the stables, Bianca had made a concerted effort to remain distant from him. Emotionally and physically. The first fortnight at Halverstone, she'd nearly succumbed to his charm, but renewed determination fueled by fear of what would happen to her if she failed had firmed her resolve.

Casting a glance at the tall window, Bianca yawned and stretched. A sliver of sunlight filtered through the small gap between the rose damask draperies.

Another splendid day.

She might as well rise and go for her morning walk. She'd missed Pierce's company this past week, but it was for the best. To be honest, she'd rather stay here with him. But such a thing was improbable and impossible.

They'd have us wed in a trice, repeated in her head so often that it had become an annoying chant. Bianca suspected his sisters would approve of a union between her and their wayward brother. Probably because she was so staunch on propriety, and he just the opposite. Little did they know the wicked thoughts she entertained about him.

He'd stayed at Halverstone far longer than she'd anticipated, and she fully expected he'd be off to London any day to resume his pleasure-seeking lifestyle. A rueful smile curved her mouth. Despite that truth, she'd longed for his company. Longed for more as he'd promised she would.

She glanced at his door.

Was he awake yet?

She squinted at the clock in the dim light.

Not quite six yet.

Probably not, then.

At eleven last night, when she'd crept downstairs to borrow a book from the library, candlelight had still glowed beneath the study door. Before she heard him moving about in his room, the rather dull story had lulled her to sleep.

Bianca swung her legs over the edge of the bed, then paused to pet the cat. "You'll not be sleeping here when your babies arrive. Everything I own will be covered in cat hair."

Miss Millie purred on, her different colored eyes half-closed in contentment as she kneaded the down coverlet. Her distended belly proclaimed that kittens would soon join the household.

A few minutes later, after cleansing her teeth, washing her face, and twisting her unruly hair into a simple knot, Bianca donned her humblest gown. A cow had given birth yesterday, and she wanted to visit the newborn.

Since Pierce still slept, she needn't worry about appearing a frump.

No coins clinked within the frock's hidden pocket. As clever as she thought she'd been, someone had discovered her paltry stash. Without those funds, Bianca had no choice but to remain at Halverstone until she won her wager with Pierce.

Would he truly let her go?

He'd never actually said so.

Bianca pushed those misgivings to the back of her mind. Everything hinged on his permitting her to return to Elmswood.

Her worn but practical walking boots, an equally shabby cloak, and plain straw bonnet, somewhat frayed about the edges, came next. Lastly, she collected her leather gloves. Actually, they had been Uncle Sylvester's, but they possessed a bit of life in them yet. And as the cost of kid gloves was dearer than she could afford, she wore the too big gloves for more earthy tasks.

Such as petting adorable calves and saying hello to Luna, too.

She'd ridden the mare three times, but since Pierce always insisted on accompanying her, Bianca had forsworn the pleasure.

Glimpsing herself in the floor-length cheval mirror, she pulled a face.

A crofter's wife.

That was what she looked like. Not that there was

anything wrong with that humble but decent position. She'd just much rather look a mite more elegant.

Bianca gave the cat another pat, then slipped from her chamber, her gaze migrating of its own accord to Pierce's bedchamber door.

Despite her determination not to, she'd fallen far under his spell already. Just three weeks, and she'd sunk faster than a cannonball-blasted schooner.

"Only a few more days. I can do it. I must. I shall not end up like Mum," Bianca muttered to herself as she descended the stairs.

"Miss, how am I supposed to be your lady's maid when you're dressed and your room tidied before I come up in the mornings?" Hands on her hips and sporting a wide grin, Elsie stood at the bottom of the staircase and shook her head in its bob cap.

Bianca would never grow accustomed to others doing for her what she was capable of doing herself. "I didn't make my bed yet this morning because Miss Millie's asleep atop it. Does that make you happy?"

"I'm supposed to help you too, Miss." Elsie still wore a contagious smile as she passed Bianca on the risers. "Though I have to admit, Mrs. Digby keeps me running. Don't know how they managed before I came."

They didn't have their master and his ward's needs to fuss about.

"All the more reason I should continue tending to myself." Bianca checked the frayed frogs at her throat, then drew on a glove. "Have you any idea how Miss Millie keeps getting into my chamber?"

One hand on the banister, Elsie knitted her forehead.

"No, Miss. The door is closed at night. After I bank the fire, I make sure of it. I'll check your room again and see if there's another way she's getting inside." Her expression cleared, and she clasped her hands to her chest. "I cannot wait for her to have her babies. Mrs. Digby says I might claim a kitten for my own. I'm hoping for an orange and white male. I'm going to name him Marmalade."

Pulling on her other glove, Bianca eyed her. She didn't want to crush Elsie's enthusiasm, but had Pierce agreed? "Won't his lordship have a say in that? I didn't see any cats in his London townhouse."

"Oh, I'm going to remain here. Mrs. Digby asked me to, and m'lord agreed. I like the country much better than London. It's cleaner and smells nicer." Elsie's smile slipped a notch, concern crimping the perimeter of her round face. "I thought you knew."

"I think that's a splendid notion. And I, too, prefer the country, truth to tell. Though London does have a few attractions I should still like to see once. I've heard Vauxhall and Covent Gardens are spectacular at night—like fairylands ablaze with light. The Theatre Royal, Bullock's Museum, and Gunter's Ices are others that spring to mind straight off."

Bertram had denied her any excursions while they were in London. No coin to spare on frivolities. However, he considered cigars, spirits, and gambling—*probably strumpets too*—absolute necessities.

With a small wave, Bianca finished descending the stairs.

So far, the additional help that Pierce mentioned hiring hadn't appeared, except for the two brawny chaps who'd arrived last week. Honestly, she didn't think

Halverstone required more servants. She preferred the intimacy of a smaller household. It gave the manor a cozier atmosphere.

After spending ten minutes with the darling, chocolaty-eyed heifer, Bianca made her way to Luna's stall. "Hello, lovely."

Luna nickered and blew her breath into Bianca's face.

"Yes, I've brought you a treat, but I'm afraid there'll be no outing for either of us. I am truly sorry." Bianca fed the mare the carrots and then, with a final pat on her withers, collected the basket of stale bread she'd picked up in the kitchen.

A while later, she stood on the pond's small dock, tossing pieces onto the water. For weeks, she'd attempted to coax the ducks to come near her and eat. Cautious creatures, they always waited until she left to paddle over and gobble the treat.

Wistfulness grasped her.

In a few days, she'd leave this place and never return. Doubtless never see Pierce again either. At least not in this informal capacity. Sorrow wrenched a small sigh from her as an intense pain she couldn't put a name to cramped her lungs.

"I thought I might find you here. I know few women who part with their beds as early as you do."

She started and swung around to find, a mere three feet away, the man who intruded upon her musings far too often.

"Goodness. I didn't hear you approach, Pierce."

"The grass muffled my footsteps." He hitched his mouth up on one side and extended his hand, palm upward, as he stepped onto the wooden planks. His extra weight caused the rowboat moored there to rock. "May I?"

"Of course." She handed him a few morsels. "They are quite timid yet."

He pointed to the boat.

"Would you like to go for a row one day? We could take bread with us too. Perhaps they'd feel safer in the middle." He glanced at the startling blue sky. "Digby says Bewick's swans often winter here."

"Oh, I should love to see them. I've always adored swans, though I've only seen one pair once and never wild ones." She glanced at the stately house. "I think Halverstone must be lovely in the winter. Especially covered with snow, though I don't imagine that happens often."

"I honestly don't know. I've always spent my winters in London. We could winter here if you'd like to. Have a proper Christmastide." Pierce aimed, then threw a crust to an emerald-headed drake.

Was that a wistful note in his voice?

Surely not.

Besides, Christmas was months away. She would leave within days. Only she didn't want to any longer.

Bianca gave him a sideways look. Nothing about his profile suggested he was waxing melancholy. And why should he, for pity's sake?

When she didn't answer, he tossed another scrap into the smooth water. It floated there, slowly swirling 'round and 'round.

"I hope you won't object, Bianca, but I've arranged

for an excursion for us today."

"Oh? Where to?"

The neighbors, the Duke and Duchess of Dandridge?

Drat.

What would she wear to cause him the least embarrassment?

The moss—*drab*—green or the slate—*cigar-ash-gray*—day dress?

Both turned her skin sallow and hung loosely at her waist. She'd lost weight in recent days, her appetite as fickle as her bothersome emotions.

"Northhollow is but six miles from here, and the Digbys have made a list of supplies that need purchasing or ordering. I also want to post an advert for additional staff. And I thought while we were there, we could see about a wardrobe for you.

"The village cannot boast London's fashionable modistes and milliners, but if my memory serves, there are at least two dressmakers. I also need to post a few letters."

He threw the rest of his bread into the water, then rubbed his palms together, ridding them of any lingering crumbs. "I'd hoped to hear something from the Chancery Court by now, truth to tell."

She had too, and the not knowing proved burdensome.

A dove dipped and wove its way across the sky to alight on a birch branch farther along the shore of the pond. It cocked its grayish-brown head and cooed. Somewhere nearby, another dove answered.

Bianca brushed her hands off, too.

"If I understood Mrs. Garside, the Chancery Court is notoriously plodding when it comes to rulings. Which is why I am here, is it not, my lord? To give the court time to make a ruling while I'm hiding from Bertram?"

"You've used my given name for weeks, and now it's back to 'my lord'?"

Pierce tucked her hand into his elbow as if it were an old habit, totally ignoring her question about the Chancery Court and her cousin.

"Yes, well," she said, trying—*unsuccessfully*—not

to notice his muscular bicep straining against his tailored coat. "We should strive to keep our relationship within the bounds of propriety. You are an earl, and I am—"

"A descendant of James II. I'm sure that makes us most compatible."

What an odd choice of words.

"Actually, I've never found any evidence to support that claim, Pierce. I suspect if it is true, and I have begun to sincerely doubt that it is, then I'm from the wrong side of the blanket. Which makes me even less acceptable."

He gave her a saucy wink, and Bianca clamped her teeth against her instinct to smile.

"Well, I'm only half English. My mother was a Munda princess from East India." A sliver of defiance colored his last words.

Bianca didn't give a fig if he was part merman or centaur or werewolf.

She angled her head. "How fascinating. I'd love to hear more about her and the Munda. I've always wanted to travel, to learn about other cultures and peoples."

Astonishment peaked Pierce's eyebrows, but his wide smile conveyed that she'd pleased him.

She ought to withdraw her hand. Touching him was most imprudent.

As if he sensed her intent, Pierce pressed his palm to the back of her hand, preventing her escape, and angled them toward the garden. On the far side, Broomfield toddled about singing off-key beneath his breath and nipping the spent blossoms.

One new fellow attended the shrubberies.

'I don't think it's appropriate for you to buy me clothing, Pierce."

"I beg to differ, Bianca. As your guardian, it *is* fitting for me to procure clothing for you."

Back to that, is he?

"You are my ward, and I take my duty to oversee your welfare seriously."

"The guardianship isn't official, may never be, as you well know. And I prefer not being obligated to you," she argued. It would make her feel like a kept woman. A mistress. "My attire is not your responsibility. I cannot permit you to clothe me."

The gesture might be misconstrued. *Might*? No, people *would* misinterpret it, no matter how innocent. The problem lay in the manner in which Pierce came into the potential guardianship, and that blot could not easily be erased from society's memory. Or hers.

"I have the paper to prove I am your guardian. You saw your cousin sign it, too." Eyes alight with confidence, he patted her arm.

Why did he have to be so blasted irresistible?

Why did she have to be so dashed responsive to him?

A small branch blocked the pathway, and she stepped over it, catching her toe on the unraveled hem of her gown. She almost stumbled, but Pierce's strong hand at her waist steadied her.

The heat from his palm burned through her cloak, gown, and chemise, clear to her skin. Rather than jerk away from the tantalizing sensation, she battled an acute desire to press into his embrace

"I mean to make it official, Bianca. One way or another, I shall assume legal responsibility for you."

One way or another?

What other way was there?

"And besides, as I mentioned before," Pierce said, "I hope to impose upon you to help with the hiring of staff and the refurbishing of Halverstone. From my observations, the kitchen gardens aren't as robust as they might be, either. Those are areas I have little experience in and which need a woman's hand."

He grinned down at her, a lock of hair falling forward and giving him a boyish demeanor.

Gone was the hardened, stone-faced man who'd won her at the gaming table.

"You may consider that payment for your new garments and other necessities if that makes you feel more proper." Pierce patted her hand. "I'm sure there are many other ways you might put your talents to use. Fairfax did say you ran an efficient household."

"Mrs. Digby might have something to say about that."

Pierce had mentioned his absence from Halverstone for almost five years, and though he was the earl and their employer, the Digbys ran the place the way they thought best. Sudden change wouldn't be well-received.

"You leave the Digbys to me, my pet."

Squinting slightly against the vivid azure framing his hatless head, she halted and searched his features. "Just how long do you plan on my staying here? Have you forgotten our wager? In a few days, I am to return to Elmswood Parke."

If I don't kiss you, that is.

She certainly wasn't going to ask for the '*more*,' no matter how curious she might be.

A hare darted across the path, and Pierce watched the sleek animal disappear into the hedgerow.

"But a lot can happen in a short period of time, my sweet. I know an earl who fell in love and married within a week. And if you recall, I never explicitly agreed to your terms."

A sudden rush of tears stung behind her lids, and she went rigid.

How could she forge her own future then? A future without a hint of scandal or dishonor.

But perhaps it was too late for that already.

He halted behind a shrub dappled with tiny dark pink flowers and drew her stiff form nearer.

"Please don't be miffed with me, sweeting."

He kissed her nose, the act so endearing that her ire dissolved.

Why did he have this effect on her?

Righteous vexation ought to be singing through her pores, not a sweet, languid sensation like warm honey.

"I've been hard-pressed not to taste your pretty mouth again. Abstaining is proving more difficult than I'd imagined." He canted his head toward the pond. "I've taken to swimming in yonder pond each evening."

He had?

Still, he would break her heart if she didn't remain resolute.

Her wayward attention strayed to the pond. The water must be frigid, even if June was upon them. Why hadn't she seen him from her balcony?

Then he must take his cold plunges after dark. Wasn't that a mite dangerous?

"Tell me you struggle against temptation as much as I, my sweet." The husky timbre of his voice caused those deuced nape hairs to perk up once again.

Bianca knew how she *should* respond, but once more, her capricious emotions betrayed her.

Dashed shilly-shallying things.

Certainly, she shouldn't feel this giddiness at his confession. Shouldn't notice how he loomed above her, making her feel protected and dainty when many men must look upward to meet her eyes. Particularly since Pierce had all but admitted he didn't intend to honor their agreement.

"Well, be assured, my lord, I have no similar inclinations to kiss you."

She presented her profile and pulled her hand from the crook of his elbow. Pray her expression didn't belie her words.

He chuckled and traced his finger along her jaw. "Liar. I see the desire in your magnificent eyes."

Indignation billowed within her lungs, and she spun to face him.

He met her fuming glare with a winning grin.

She curled her toes and gritted her teeth against a most unladylike oath.

"This is not a game, Pierce. I cannot—*shall not!*—be compromised."

She poked him in the chest just above his paisley waistcoat. "I've seen London's east end. Seen the unfortunate, once respectable women, even young girls, their circumstances reduced to desperation, plying their trade."

Bianca swallowed against the sickening tautness in her belly. Shaking her head in frustration at herself as much as at him, she firmed her lips.

"If nothing else, I'm sensible. Surrendering to a moment of ecstasy with a man I find deucedly attractive, no matter how much I might want it, simply isn't worth that risk. Not in the end."

Because her mum had surrendered to such insanity and then been left to raise a child alone. After Uncle died, Bianca found a neat stack of letters, tied with a string, buried in the bottom of his desk drawer. Mum had written him when Father had disappeared shortly before Bianca's fifth birthday.

Mum never knew what happened to Papa. Didn't know if he'd abandoned them. If he had been pressed into service aboard a ship. Or even if he'd been murdered.

One day, he'd just vanished.

As time passed, Mum's letters to Uncle Sylvester had become more infrequent and stopped altogether after a couple of years. Still, Mum had refused to move back to Elmswood. Refused to believe Papa wouldn't return someday.

Even when they'd been forced to let their housekeeper and cook go, had left their cozy house and lived in a humble paint-chipped room in a dingy part of London, she'd never given up.

What would it be like to love so profoundly?

Wholly wonderful.

Utterly horrid.

Love like that controlled a person. Stole their ability to make rational decisions.

While Mum worked, Bianca had stayed in their one-room lodging, the door locked from outside. Clutching a ragdoll, the only toy she ever owned, Bianca had watched the pitiful creatures outside begging for a crust of bread.

From the small, grungy two-paned window overlooking a street and three alleys, she'd seen other awful things an innocent child should never witness. Things that had terrified her and made her determined to never become one of those pathetic women.

In that room, Mum had taught her to read, write, and do sums, and later when Bianca grew older, the door had been kept locked from inside to keep the riffraff out.

One day when she was eight years old, Mum was late coming home. Bianca's empty stomach gnawed away at her spine, and she'd disobeyed and left the room. Scared, for she'd never walked the street alone, she hurried to the pastry shop to see what was keeping her mother.

The place had smelled divine, and her stomach had rumbled its appreciation. Only Mum didn't work there anymore. Times were hard, and she'd been dismissed over a year prior.

Such pity etched the woman's face who gently broke the news to Bianca that she'd wanted to collapse, curl into a ball, and sob right there before the counter. Instead, she'd accepted the warm roll the woman offered and returned to their hovel, having matured twenty years.

She never told Mum she'd left their room. Never told her she knew she didn't work at the bakery any longer. Never asked what she did when she left Bianca alone for hours and hours at night.

Even as a child Bianca *knew*.

Perhaps not the specifics. Nevertheless, she'd seen enough from the fusty rectangle overlooking the neighborhood to get the gist. Horror and shame kept her mute. Still kept her silent but doggedly determined to avoid the same vile fate.

Pierce captured one of the curls that escaped its

confines and wrapped it around his forefinger, drawing her back to the present. Though his tone remained light and playful, the contours of his face seemed more pronounced. "So you admit to desiring me?"

Out of all that Bianca had said, he picked that morsel to comment on?

It seemed to be a habit of his.

"Do not take me for a bacon brain. You know that I do. I cannot resist you, though God knows I try. I believe the foolish incident in the carriage made that perfectly clear."

Bianca must not submit to his magnetism. She must be unpredictable. Must keep him off his guard.

"I don't know." Pierce lazily fingered her curl. "I don't think it was so very imprudent. I rather enjoyed it."

She narrowed her eyes.

Did he speak of their kiss or her bungling attempt at seduction?

Fine. She knew just the thing to scare away a rakehell like him. He would distance himself from her so fast and so far that she needn't fear his attention any longer.

"Unless I have a band around my third finger, Pierce," she held up her hand and wiggled the appendage, "I'm not dallying with any man. Not even sinfully handsome, tempting-as-sin lords such as you."

Just when she believed she had the upper hand, he neatly turned the tables on her. His gaze locked with hers, Pierce raised her hands to his mouth and pressed his lips to them for a lengthy moment.

God help her, but she could get lost—no, she could drown in those unfathomable, black-fringed depths.

"Then marry me, my darling, sweet, obstinate, impulsive, wonderful Bianca."

11

Pierce had not planned to propose.

Yet the words spilled from his mouth, expressing what he'd contemplated for days.

Weeks.

From that first morning when she'd intruded into his bedchamber and Popplewell planted the ludicrous notion in his head. He didn't regret the impulse either. Wedding Bianca was the perfect solution. Besides, he wanted to marry this unpredictable, remarkable, delightfully aggravating woman.

Theirs would be no marriage of convenience. The part of him that delighted in thumbing his nose at tradition and expectations thrilled at that fact.

Perhaps it was an insane impulse, but she brought a part of him alive that he had long since thought dead. Or, at the very least, dormant.

They would quarrel, of that, he had no doubt.

Probably have great, fierce, bloody loud rows, truth to tell. But life wouldn't be dull or predictable married to Bianca. It had been for so long that he'd forgotten what excitement felt like—what it was to anticipate something other than revenge.

Yes, Bianca Salisbury was the perfect woman for him.

He couldn't be more certain of it. Even if he had only known her for weeks. Why, even her height suited him. The crown of her burnished head came to the juncture of his shoulder, and despite her stature, she possessed a svelte figure.

Except for her big feet.

She'd be peeved to know how much that little detail amused him. Even so, he'd vow she danced as gracefully as she walked, slight limp or no.

He kissed her knuckles again.

The moment she said yes, he would claim her scrumptious mouth, too.

"What say you?" Closing his eyes, Pierce brushed his face against her satiny cheek. "We can be married as soon as the banns are read. Or if you prefer, we can go to Scotland and skip all that formal falderal."

A most unladylike snort resounded near his ear, and he leaned away to study her face.

Something near scorn tightened Bianca's features, and amber fire flared within her gaze.

"Now you mock me." She tried to pull her hands free, her eyes luminous and wounded. "I know you have a devilish reputation, and I know you probably find me highly amusing. But I never considered you would stoop to unkindness."

"Darling, I'm perfectly earnest. The notion occurred to me days ago. And the more I've pondered it, the more I'm convinced it's the perfect solution. You need protection, Bianca, and I need a wife."

"Oh, you…you rogue." She shoved at his chest. "*Those* are your reasons for proposing?"

Her color high and those incredible eyes sparking with indignation, she'd never looked so magnificent.

He probably ought to have given her a bit more time and no have mentioned that snippet about needing a wife. But then again, Pierce never thought he'd want to marry. Nevertheless, now he did. Bianca's wit and intellect, her straightforward speech, the fact that she didn't turn all feminine fluff and guile to get her way, attracted every bit as much as her lush form.

From her glorious hair, a shiny, untamed burnished copper halo framing her face in this morning's sun, to her cherub's nose, peach-tinted mouth, and slightly overgrown feet, she fascinated him.

In fact, wonder of wonders, she'd even managed to temper his animosity toward Fairfax the merest degree.

Pierce knew full well what Coventry would say, his mouth skewed into a smug smile.

"You've fallen in love, Wainthorpe, old chap."

That carried things a trifle too far. Pierce didn't love Bianca.

Did he?

No, of course not. Love was elusive, otherworldly, fragile.

Nothing like this molten stirring he felt—powerful, strong, infiltrating every aspect of his life. For she'd taken up residence in his mind, and from the moment Bianca's gaze had pleaded with him from across the room during the card game, something unnamed had also taken root in his chest and simmered in his blood.

Her expression grew shrewd, and he felt her prodding his thoughts, trying to read them.

"It doesn't make the least sense," she muttered, her features scrunched in bewilderment. "You cannot possibly want to marry a woman such as I. Aside from barely knowing one another, I'm no beauty, and I have no dowry."

Bianca had already told Pierce about her dowry, and that she was unaware of her exquisiteness caused him a sort of sadness he couldn't quite explain.

"I don't care about a marriage settlement, and though you may not believe me, Bianca, I find you remarkable, fascinating, and utterly lovely."

Seemingly oblivious to his compliment, she shook her head again. "I haven't a doubt that you would grow bored with me within a sennight. A month at most, then put me aside and return to your horde of demimondaines. Why, you probably don't even know the number of women you've lain with, let alone remember their names."

Either disdain or disenchantment leached into her mumbled comment.

His pride shredded by her lowly opinion, he released her.

Bianca put a finger to her chin and, tilting her head to the side, regarded him.

"So what's your motivation?" As she drew herself upright, her features darkened, and comprehension lit her eyes. "Besides despising my only living kin, that is? Is *that* why?"

"That suggestion is beyond insulting and not worthy of refuting." His posture as guarded as a fortified castle, Pierce stepped away from her. "I shall put Elmswood at your disposal. I have no need for the estate. But you will remain in my care until such time as I deem it is safe for you to return there. It may be days, weeks, or even months. Those terms will have to suffice."

She gave one short nod, her naughty curls bouncing with the enthusiasm their mistress's reply lacked.

Pierce had expected a blistering retort and adamant denial—would've preferred them to her complacent response. He cast a deliberate, disparaging glance over her attire, and she notched her chin upward, silently defying him.

Ah, there was that impertinence.

He adored that about her.

"You still need decent clothes. As your guardian, I shan't have it said that I've neglected you. I've been remiss for too long in that regard as it is. The carriage will await us out front at half-past ten." Flummoxed by the anger and disillusionment surging through him, he pivoted toward the house. He took one step, then paused and angled halfway in her direction.

"'Tis true I have no love for your cousin. He's

responsible for my mother's death. But until I saw you at Lady Lockhart's, I didn't know you existed."

Bianca's mouth sagged into an 'O', her almond-shaped cinnamon eyes big and startled.

"And, Bianca, in case you're wondering, I have never asked for a woman's hand before either. I waited until I found a woman who I thought could be my equal."

Why he deemed that important enough to share with her, Pierce couldn't quite say. Perhaps he simply wanted her to know that though he'd bedded other women, he'd saved proposing until he met a woman who stirred something more than his libido.

With that, he strode across the green, humiliation stabbing him between the shoulders with each peeved step. At long last, not out of obligation or duty, but because he truly wanted to, he'd proposed to the only woman ever to capture his interest, not merely his lust.

And Bianca threw the offer back in his face. No, she heaved it onto the ground and stomped upon it, even intimating that he'd planned this debacle to ruin her.

He'd only ever been trying to protect her.

Why couldn't she understand that?

What was she so afraid of?

For the first time in decades, hot moisture pricked Pierce's eyes, and he blinked several times to clear them. How was it bloody possible to care for her so much in such a short while? Care that she'd refused his suit? Care what she thought of him and that her scorn and rejection could turn him into a leaky-eyed milksop?

Surely, this unbearable ripping apart behind his ribs was not love.

Bianca was wrong, too.

He would *never* become bored with her, and he could too remember the five women's names he'd ever been intimate with.

AamA used to tell him everyone had a soul mate, and those fortunate enough to find theirs sometimes knew instantly they'd found the other half to their souls. She claimed it was so with her and Father. He'd been considerably older, and though of different ethnicities, religions, social status, and even political persuasions, she swore none of those things mattered.

She gave Father her heart and soul, and he did the same without regret.

For over eight years, they'd been blissful. True, Father's work as a diplomat and his title and three daughters took him back to England quite regularly. *AamA* refused to accompany him, declaring she would be as out of place in his home country as a rhinoceros in a chocolate shop. Yet, they'd been happy. Even their spats about her involvement in the resistance against English rule couldn't warp their love.

From time to time, the trio vowed similar sentimental drivel, though none of their matches were an idyllic love-at-first-sight phenomenon.

No, as Pierce deliberated about it, each of his sister's unions were fraught with misunderstandings and complications. And yet, his brothers-in-law, each formerly as much a rapscallion as he, enjoyed wedded paradise now.

Maybe that love codswallop had some merit after all.

Unable to resist, Pierce glanced over his shoulder.

Bianca stood exactly where he'd left her. Staring into the distance, her shoulders hunched in dejection, she hugged herself. It was impossible to tell for certain from here with the sunlight bathing her, but dampness appeared to glisten on her cheeks.

Maybe all she needed was more time. More courting, too.

Elsie might be of some help in that regard. Perchance the servant knew a thing or two about her mistress that Pierce didn't, which could prove useful.

Truth be known, Pierce *had* rushed things a trifle.

More to the point, Bianca must trust him. Trust that no ulterior motives had induced him to offer for her. Hopefully, that would lay a foundation for redeeming himself. Because if he failed…

Without her, he faced a dismal, hollow existence.

Pierce wasn't ready to quit the field after losing the first battle. He would stay and make a valiant effort not to mope about, a love-struck swain, his pride be hanged.

~*~

No wonder Pierce hated Bertram.

Bianca would hate him, too.

Anguish kept her immobile as she stared across the lake, tears wetting her cheeks.

Only Pierce possessed the ability to turn her into a dribbly fountain, blast him. Although she wanted to reject the reason why, her logical mind denied her the privilege.

She was falling in love.

Maybe had already completely done so, and lost herself, lost sight of her destiny in the process. More maddeningly, she didn't want to be conflicted—wanted the decision, the path forward to be obvious. But love wasn't obvious or easy, either.

Not at all.

This glorious hurt, this willingness to be vulnerable, knowing the person you've given your very soul to could shatter it into countless shards with a callous glance, a cutting gesture, or a slicing word was agony at its acutest.

Mum had loved like that, and her adoration eventually crushed her. But if Bianca married Pierce, at least her physical wellbeing would be assured.

She released a scornful laugh that ended on a strangled sob.

Now she was entertaining the ludicrous notion?

Sighing, she shoved her loose curls behind her ears and kicked a rock into the pond. It did little to ease her melancholy.

The ducks, their shoe-button black eyes regarding her warily, swam in slow circles, quacking occasionally. On the other side of the pond, a duck paddled to the edge, then waddled ashore. Five downy, black and yellow ducklings followed her.

Despite Bianca's doldrums, she turned her mouth upward at the precious little fluff balls scurrying and quacking behind their mum.

Another unbidden sigh whisked past her lips.

The peril of a woman possessing her nature was that she would never cease loving Pierce. Even when he gravitated back to his sirens and gaming hells. Like a faithful dog that comes back and licks her master's hand even after he kicks her, she would love him.

Only an utter nit-wit fell tail feathers over teapot spout in love with a known philanderer.

In less than a month, too.

Such rashness guaranteed a broken heart.

For a man like Pierce, she was sorely tempted to take that chance. It might be worth it, just for the few memories she would have.

No! It wouldn't, her common sense berated.

No, it wouldn't.

It would ravage her.

~*~

That afternoon, Bianca directed Elsie where to put the ready-made items Pierce had purchased for her in Northhollow. The rest of her wardrobe would not be completed for two weeks.

She'd only permitted him to order three morning

gowns, an equal number of day dresses, and one ivory spencer she might wear with any of them. He'd inquired about a gown appropriate for evening wear, and Bianca's eyes nearly boggled from her head when the shop owner murmured the garment's cost.

Always frugal, Bianca had tried to stand her ground and proclaimed her current shift and chemise were perfectly good. She didn't need any more.

Pierce, however, cocked a superior raven brow and proceeded to order two of each for her as well as several pairs of stockings, slippers, and even stays.

"Lenora said you improvised with bed linens, and as much as I admire your ingenuity and economy, Bianca, your new gowns demand new underthings as well."

At his reminder of her intimate apparel, another scorching blush suffused her.

No surprise that he knew a woman's wardrobe from the skin outward. But to think that he and his sisters actually believed she'd fashioned undergarments from old linens brought a new surge of chagrin.

She ought not to have jested about that, but Bianca had so wanted to shock Miss Walcott.

Although Mrs. Dunlap hadn't uttered so much as a syllable in suspicion, her skeptical, forced smile had hinted at her disbelief when Pierce introduced Bianca as his ward. The flush skimming from Bianca's neck to her hairline mightn't have helped dissuade the dressmaker's inaccurate assumption either.

Even this far removed from London, their relationship raised speculation. That hadn't stopped the seamstress from eagerly presenting fripperies and fallalls as well as her most current fashion plates.

"An earl is an earl, after all. If his lordship desires to purchase a wardrobe for a young lady, it isn't my place to question his reasons," the dressmaker mumbled beneath her breath while measuring Bianca's waist.

She only dared such impudence because Pierce had left them to run his errands.

Elsie sniffed one of the new floral embossed oval soaps, then rewrapped it in tissue paper.

"I don't think I've ever smelled anything as

wonderful. Would you like a bath before dinner, miss? You could also take a short nap. You were up so early this morning. I could make you a cup of chamomile tea as well."

So she'd seen the yawn Bianca attempted to hide behind her hand.

"You can wear your new gown, too. It's just his lordship and you dining, so it's no matter that it's a day gown. Especially since it's the finest in your wardrobe." Her round face crumpled, and her cheeks glowed raspberry red when she realized her gaffe. "I meant no disrespect, Miss."

"I know you didn't. And yes, a bath and the tea would be lovely."

A lengthy soak and the soothing brew did appeal. It might help alleviate the headache brought on by hours of measurements and pinning. As tempted as Bianca was to request a tray sent to her chamber tonight, she wasn't a coward. She'd face Pierce across the table and answer his inquires with the same aloofness he'd presented to her the entire day.

Several times throughout the morning and afternoon, Bianca opened her mouth to ask exactly how Bertram had caused Pierce's mother's death. Yet each time, her manners refused to allow her to pry into something so personal and obviously painful.

If he wanted her to know, he'd tell her.

He was as entitled to his secrets as she was to hers.

12

Boots crunching in the gravel, Pierce trod the meandering garden path, occasionally nodding his approval to Broomfield and what the staff thought were two newly hired hands. They were in fact, old acquaintances. Men who specialized in covert security, and their purpose was to protect Bianca.

Not that he worried overly much about Fairfax fighting the guardianship now. Reflecting over these past weeks, he'd concluded Fairfax wouldn't want the expense of caring for Bianca again.

Nevertheless, Felix and Chambers, a slight sardonic bend to their mouths, dutifully worked at putting the finishing touches on Pierce's surprise for Bianca.

Digby, Elsie, the other two maids, Burroughs, and even Popplewell had put aside their normal duties to help as well.

Given his valet's cross scowl, Popplewell believed the task beneath him. Yet he humored his employer. Not without a considerable amount of grumbling, however. Unlike good-natured Mrs. Digby in the kitchen, preparing another surprise at Pierce's behest.

Elsie gave a little one-handed wave as he passed.

"Miss Bianca's resting, just like we planned, m'lord."

At first, the loyal, closed-lipped maid hadn't been eager to share what she knew about her mistress. When Pierce explained he wanted to do something special for Bianca, Elsie had chattered on like a magpie.

"Excellent. Thank you for your help, Elsie," he said.

She dimpled and turned her attention back to the bush she was adorning.

Call Pierce a codpate, but he'd decided to court Bianca full on. She'd become as essential as air and water, as addicting as opium, and he craved her presence. Her love. If he didn't succeed in winning her…

No.

This quest had only just begun in earnest. He would not harbor a single thought about defeat. Not at this early juncture, anyway.

A disturbance on the pond drew his attention.

A drake had chased another male away from a hen. Pierce well understood the possessive sentiment. He grinned and touched his scar. There might be something to that nonsensical soul mate stuff his mother had rattled on about after all.

Self-castigation, or perhaps irony, better described the feeling infusing him. He'd finally admitted the truth to himself this afternoon. Actually, while he'd watched Bianca, her shoulders and chin set in resolution, tolerate Mrs. Dunlap's ministrations.

What a marvelous revelation, too.

By Jove, he'd succumbed to the unthinkable, the wonderfully untenable, and given his heart to the fiery vixen. Now he would do almost anything to make Bianca his countess and, one day, his duchess.

Hands clasped behind his back, he surveyed his property. Yonder beech tree possessed ideal branches for a rope swing or two.

He and Bianca would have four offspring: an ebony-haired boy and girl like him and a ginger-haired boy and girl like her. And a cat and a dog, too. And ponies for their children. Maybe even a parakeet. As a child, he'd seen the winged green clouds spiraling through the hazy India skies and wanted one.

Unfamiliar giddiness soared behind his breastbone, and he chuckled. He'd become a besotted fool. He, the acerbic, unemotional Earl of Wainthorpe.

He envisioned Coventry's smug grin as he announced that another member of the Wicked Earls' Club had succumbed to love's indefensible allure. Is that what he meant when he'd chortled that Pierce "…didn't realize the truth of it?"

Marching across the lawn, Pierce glanced at Bianca's balcony windows. The drawn draperies hid the hectic preparations outside, all part of Elsie's subterfuge to assist Pierce.

Whistling a tune he'd heard Bianca singing yesterday, he cast a final glance around the lawns and gardens. Satisfied with the progress, he entered his study by way of the terrace. Stacked atop his desk lay the post he'd collected in Northhollow.

Mayhap it contained some word of Fairfax's whereabouts.

Most well-bred misses—all that Pierce was acquainted with—were ignorant of the seedier parts of London, much less knew about the atrocities that went on there. That Bianca did, made him more than a little curious. So, before he bundled her off to Halverstone, he also asked Simmons to do a bit of discreet poking about to see what he could discover regarding Bianca's mother. While he was at it, he asked Simmons to make inquiries about her father too.

Men didn't just vanish.

Someone knew something.

Sinking into his button-tufted leather chair, he lifted the top letter and quirked his mouth.

From Simmons.

Pray it contained good news. He cracked the seal with his thumbnail. Touching two fingers to his scar, he read the letter, concentration pulling his eyebrows tight. Once finished, he sighed and tossed the missive atop his desk.

Chock-full of news, mostly unsavory and unpleasant.

Information he'd have to tell Bianca, including a diary of her uncle's that Churchgrove had found at Elmswood that evidently revealed much. But not tonight. Tonight was for her. Resting his chin on his steepled fingertips, Pierce sank back into the chair.

Unlike three weeks ago, no satisfaction thrummed through him. In fact, if he put a name to what he most felt at the moment, it would have to be pity. Not even Fairfax deserved to have his throat slit—his body tossed into the Thames for fish food.

His corpse had been discovered a week ago.

It seemed he'd borrowed from the same unscrupulous moneylender once too often.

~*~

Just before the clock struck seven, after a soothing bath, calming tea, and a lie down, Bianca stood before the full-length mirror once more.

Was that really her?

The serene, fashionably dressed and coiffed woman gazing back at her didn't much resemble the farmer's wife who'd trundled to the barn this morning to pet a sweet calf. All she lacked were emeralds to match the gown or perhaps jets at her ears, throat, and wrist to be a proper *tonnish* lady.

The toes of her black shoes, a startling contrast against the gown's lovely silk fabric, caused her to purse her mouth. Pierce had ordered her pretty slippers and a pair of half-boots as well.

Mrs. Dunlap couldn't mask her astonishment at the size of Bianca's feet.

Bianca lifted a leg, twisting her foot this way and that.

Miniature boats. That was what she claimed for

feet.

Naught to be done about that.

However, she did wish for a delicate fragrance made especially for her by Floris's in London to dab at her wrists and behind each ear. It wouldn't hurt to have every weapon at her disposal to snare herself an earl.

For during her nap, she'd dreamed of her parents. Mum had cupped Bianca's cheeks and told her to trust her heart. Then Papa was there, embracing her, his blue eyes sparkling with tenderness.

"Always choose love, me darlin'. Always."

Bianca awoke with the most peculiar sense she'd actually been with them. She tried to shove aside her misgivings about Pierce, about a future with him, but years of fears shackled her in uncertainty. Optimism battled with doubt in her heart for a few moments more.

Then, with a final wrench, she shook herself free of her reservations and determined to heed her parents' advice. Love was too precious to be disregarded or discarded.

Minutes later, she entered the dining room as she

did every evening. Instead of being seated opposite Pierce tonight, a place setting lay to his right. Apparently, he hadn't given up wooing her just yet.

Wonderful.

Now if only he'd propose again, and Bianca could give him the answer he'd wanted this morning. A little tremor ran through her, but she schooled her features into nonchalance while chiding her undisciplined pulse to calm itself.

Pierce rose, his dark as night eyes shining with renewed appreciation at her elegant attire. "That color is most becoming on you."

"Thank you."

A perfectly proper compliment, so why did disappointment clench behind her ribs that he hadn't said something a trifle more teasing or risqué? For his scorching gaze certainly hinted at something deliciously scandalous

"Have I mentioned that green is my favorite color?" He gazed at her expectantly, like a little boy eagerly sharing a secret with his best friend.

Oh, did he want to know her favorite color?

How utterly irresistible.

"Mine is dark pink. Which does not work at all with this hair." She fluttered her fingers over her carefully arranged curls.

"I think you would be beautiful wearing any color, sweeting."

He stood behind her chair, an encouraging, not the least suggestive smile creasing his face. "I've taken the liberty of having you seated beside me. I thought we ought to get to know one another properly, and bellowing down the table's length didn't appeal."

She already knew he slept naked as a newborn babe and that a coal-black, very attractive beard covered his jaw in the morning. *And smatters his magnificent chest and torso, too.* She also knew he looked dashing, even with his midnight hair disheveled, and he owned a lazy smile that made her insides wobble.

Something of her train of thought must have shown, for Pierce flashed his typical rakish smile, then patted the back of her chair. "Come. To honor your Scot's heritage, I've asked Mrs. Digby to prepare something special for you tonight."

Pierce actually remembered that little detail about her parentage?

Bianca didn't recall mentioning it to him.

And he'd actually conferred with Mrs. Digby about the menu? My, full of surprises this evening, wasn't he?

His charm proved contagious nonetheless, and Bianca returned his jaunty grin.

"May I ask what we are to dine upon?" She slipped onto the chair, all too aware of him standing behind her, his clean male scent, sandalwood and cedar, teasing her nose.

Pierce pressed his hands to her shoulders for the briefest instant after pushing her chair in. When his warm palms cupped her, his thumbs brushing her nape, she almost dropped her serviette as an electric jolt sluiced down her arms and spinal cord.

Taking his seat, he conjured that dastardly charming grin again.

Bianca pressed a palm to her middle on the pretense

of arranging the linen square. A pair of rowdy kittens frolicked in her stomach.

Did her smile cause the same riot inside him?

He lifted his serviette and, as he unfolded it, confessed, "Well, truth to tell, on such short notice, Mrs. Digby could only manage a Scot's dessert, cranachan."

"That's my favorite." Aunt Florencia always prepared the delicacy for Bianca's birthday and at Christmastide. And that Pierce went to such effort to please her made that squishy feeling in Bianca's middle spread outward until her whole body fairly hummed.

A nonplussed expression flitted across his aristocratic face's planes. "I hoped to surprise you."

"You have, and your thoughtfulness is rather endearing." She lifted the wine glass to her mouth, gazing at him across the crystal rim.

My, this flirting business came quite naturally.

"Is it now?" Pure masculine confidence oozed from Pierce.

Oh dear, oh dear.

She'd seen that penetrating expression before.

Sudden heat encompassed Bianca from the scorching stare he leveled her, dampening her palms and underarms. She hadn't bothered with a fan this evening, either. Was it possible to melt from a man's gaze? For she was nigh on to dissolving in her chair.

"Let's share a few things about ourselves, shall we? I'll go first." Pierce scratched his cheek in an almost bashful gesture. That unexpected vulnerability made her curious even as it snared her tighter in his entrancing web.

"All right, though I assure you, my life isn't nearly as colorful or as shocking as yours." Bianca could've bitten her loose tongue off for venturing into that particular arena.

Pierce merely skewed his mouth into a tolerant little half-smile. "As you know, I have three older sisters."

"Yes, the interfering trio." Bianca chuckled.

She would've adored having a sister or a brother.

"Precisely," he agreed. "I also have eleven nieces and nephews, and unless I'm off my mark, Amanda is breeding again." He gave her a closed-mouth smile.

"I'm particularly fond of children."

Another mark in his favor.

"I was born in India, inherited my title when I was eight, and I have several cousins who'd just as soon I hadn't. My closest friends are the Duke of Sutcliffe, the Earls of Pembroke and Benton, and Halverstone's nearest neighbor, the Duke of Dandridge."

Bianca suspected Pierce rarely shared in this manner. Surely that he did lent credence to his declaration that morning.

"I prefer sweetened coffee to tea, smoke an occasional cheroot, and have sworn off any spirit stronger than claret." A self-castigating grimace accompanied that disclosure. "I cannot abide pheasant, goose, or clams, but I have a fondness for rice pudding. It reminds me of a favorite Indian dessert, *payasam*, which my mother used to make. And most of the scandalous chatter you've heard about me is a calculated facade I've contrived and propagated purely to shock the *ton*."

It was?

A slow, elated smile lifted the corners of her mouth, and giddiness fluttered about her breastbone. Why did that make her inordinately pleased?

"How did your mother die?" Bianca blurted the question that had beleaguered her thoughts all day and immediately regretted her lack of control.

Pierce's smile faded, and he regarded her with that blank expression his friends teased him about.

Botheration.

Now was not the time for her usual directness. Remorse jabbed where happiness had frolicked but moments ago. She'd ruined the moment. Possibly the evening as well.

"I ought not to have asked, Pierce. It's none of my concern. Please forgive me."

A flicker of something, resignation perhaps, gleamed around his irises, and he rubbed his fingers across his forehead.

"To put it as succinctly as possible, she was killed during a Munda uprising. Which she not only sympathized with but, unbeknownst to my father, aided in the plotting. Your cousin was Captain Normand back then and a soldier in the troops sent to subdue the rebels. My mother tried to shoot him when our house was raided. An informant had outed her."

Ragged emotion deepened his melodic baritone.

His tortured expression and raspy voice nearly undid Bianca. Why couldn't she control her confounded tongue? Now he was reliving the horror, thanks to her.

"I'm so sorry." On her lap, the serviette, now fisted into a ball, suffered from her remorse.

Pierce had become so caught up in his recollection that he didn't seem to hear her.

"They wrestled for the gun. I tried to help by biting his hand. Somewhere in the midst of the struggle, the blunderbuss fired. I had one of Normand's—Fairfax's—hands clamped between my teeth. He clubbed me with the pistol's butt, giving me this." Pierce pointed to the scar above his right temple. "When I awoke, I found my mother. Dying."

"Oh, Pierce." Tears pooled, blurring Bianca's vision.

He peered across the room, lost in the painful memory. "I didn't realize at first that she'd been shot in the side. I've wondered ever since if my attacking Normand caused the gun to fire."

He glanced up, and the desolation in his ebony eyes raked Bianca's heart raw.

"Am I as much to blame for my mother's death as Fairfax?"

13

"No, Pierce. No, of course you aren't."

Bianca swallowed the constriction in her throat. She could imagine the guilt that must've plagued him all these years. "You were but a child trying to protect her."

Such a flood of sympathy for the little boy who'd seen his mother die and the man who yet blamed himself for her death overwhelmed Bianca; it was all she could do not to succumb to tears.

I shall not cry, she repeated over and over in her head.

Purring loudly, her tail a proud rudder in the air, Miss Millie wandered into the dining room and made straight for Pierce.

Bianca seized the opportunity to compose herself. She took a sip of wine and breathed in several steadying breaths.

Making little chirrup sounds, Miss Millie disappeared under the table, no doubt rubbing her scent on his feet and calves. That cat was white-whiskers-over-mottled-tail besotted.

"Miss Millie is quite enamored of you," Bianca remarked, grateful for the distraction.

"It's embarrassing, how much so." Pierce appeared as relieved as she to have the subject changed. Having restored his emotions to their usual stoic state, he peeked beneath the tablecloth. "I expect to find her curled up in my study or on my bed with several wriggling kittens any day now."

A moment later, Bianca smiled as Digby placed a bowl of soup before her.

Pierce dipped his spoon into the creamed leek and potato soup. "She follows me into my bedchamber every night and then proceeds to make herself comfortable at the foot of my bed where a thorough grooming session commences."

His bed?

A suspicion formed, so improbable, Bianca could hardly fathom it.

No, it wasn't conceivable.

She'd given Mrs. Digby the key herself, and more than once over the past several days, she'd tested the handle of the connecting door. It was locked tight every time.

But wasn't it possible Pierce possessed another key?

Well, of course it was. Not only possible but probable.

For juniper's sake, why hadn't Bianca considered that before?

Had Pierce entered her room while she slumbered?

Had he kissed her?

Why did the notion thrill rather than miff?

He took a sip of wine. "You don't like the soup?"

"No. I mean, yes. It's delicious."

Spooning the creamy mixture into her mouth, Bianca scrutinized his face. She couldn't detect any sign of guilt.

He winced, then flicked a finger at Digby. "Would you mind taking Miss Millie to the kitchen? She's decided my calf makes an ideal claw sharpener. Which is why she isn't permitted to sleep atop my bed. My legs would look like giant pin cushions."

"Of course, sir."

His expression unreadable, Digby lifted the very pregnant cat into his arms. Eyes half-closed, she gazed up at him, her rumblings undisturbed. Before he made the dining room entrance, the servant sneezed thrice.

"Poor man," Bianca said. "He shouldn't carry her about. I think he has a metabolic intolerance for cats."

"Perhaps, but Digby spoils her as much as his wife. I caught him calling Miss Millie *Pretty Puss* this morning while feeding her a chicken leg and petting her."

Setting her spoon down, Bianca cocked her head, listening for Digby's heavy tread down the corridor to the kitchen. When it faded, she pointed her finger at Pierce.

"You've been entering my chamber whilst I sleep,

haven't you?"

Spoon half-raised to his mouth, Pierce glanced upward.

"Ah, that." He lifted a shoulder. "You cry out in your sleep sometimes. You mumble quite a lot, too."

"Balderdash. I most certainly do not," Bianca denied.

No one had ever mentioned such things to her. But then again, who would've heard her? True, she endured nightmares as a child because of the awful things she'd seen and heard through the window in that too-small room of her childhood home. But she had long since stopped suffering from them.

Hadn't she?

Truth to tell, while under the same roof as Bertram, most nights, sleep hadn't come easily. She'd often awaken, her heart hammering and fear squeezing her lungs.

Pierce took a sip of soup, not the least concerned he'd been found out. "How do you know, my sweet? You're asleep."

He had her there. Nonetheless, he'd overstepped

the bounds by entering her bedchamber.

And if he'd kissed her, then he'd lost their bet.

Only how could she prove it?

"You make the cutest little snuffling noises, too." He was obviously enjoying himself at the expense of her composure.

Bianca gaped before collecting her wits. He'd find his head on the receiving end of a salt shaker should he utter another ungentlemanly word on the subject.

"Well, you probably snore like a rhino," Bianca finally retorted.

Not so much as a grunt had carried to her chamber from his side of the wall during the night.

"There's one way for you to find out for certain, Bianca, isn't there?"

"And what would that be?"

He gave her a devilish wink and a chuckle so seductive that gooseflesh raised up from her neck to her waist.

"Marry me and share my bed."

Good heavens. Temptation wasn't just knocking. It had seized a battering ram to destroy her defenses.

Did Pierce jest, or was his rejoinder a backhanded way of asking her again?

She sent a swift glance toward the kitchen entrance. No Digby yet.

She might as well ask. "Is that another proposal?"

Instead of answering, Pierce trailed his intense gaze over her face, down the length of her neck, across her shoulders, then dipped to her cleavage swelling above her bodice before meeting her eyes once more. Every single place he'd touched with his eyes tingled as if he'd caressed her with his fingertips.

Hands flat on the table on either side of her plate, she leaned forward and whispered,

"Surely you know the scandal that would ensue if you were found out, Pierce. I'd be compromised beyond redemption."

"I've considered that. But my staff knows I demand their loyalty and their discretion." Lounging against his chair, his long fingers encircling his wine glass, the signet ring on his little finger glowing from the candlelight, he murmured, "Besides, Bianca, I do care for your repute. I've been most fastidious about ensuring I am not discovered."

Bianca raised a doubtful brow and took a long drink of her wine, her nerves so strained that an entire bottle wouldn't calm the prickly sensation. Annoyance wasn't what was making her so on edge either. Her lurid imagination kept meandering to what he'd looked like abed, all disheveled manly virility, and then to his provocative comment about sharing that very same bed.

She always did have an overly vivid imagination.

Think of something else. Anything else.

Miss Millie. Yes.

Mention of the cat ought to wipe that sexy, thought-jumbling smile off his face.

For all of his confidence, Pierce hadn't been careful enough. "You needn't look so smug. You've overlooked one very important detail during your nocturnal sojourns."

He set his glass down, a crease over the bridge of his nose drawing his striking brows together. "I don't believe I have."

"Oh, but you *have*. Every time you've hurled propriety aside and entered my chamber unbeknownst to me, Miss Millie sneaked in. I'd find her on my bed the next morning, using *my* legs for a pincushion."

"She did?" That gave Pierce pause, and he slanted his attention to the empty doorway through which she'd been carried. "Why, the sly little vixen."

At his utterly confounded expression, Bianca laughed. Where was the exasperation she ought to be feeling?

"You should see yourself, Pierce. You had no idea?"

"None. I thought she was asleep under my bed."

He gave her a lopsided, apologetic smile, and her heart flopped about, the dratted, weak, gullible organ.

"Popplewell fashioned a cozy box with a blanket for her," Pierce said. "Sneaky girl. She knows I shan't permit her on my mattress, so she creeps into your room when I open the door." Contriteness accented the lines at the outer corners of his eyes.

"I was but concerned for you, Bianca. It's only happened … What? Four …? Five times?"

"Try twelve." A dozen times, he'd crept into her room and observed her sleeping.

Shouldn't she be shaking in outrage?

Bianca was quite certain this bewildering sensation pummeling her wasn't anything of the sort.

"Twelve? That many?" The planes Pierce's face stood out starkly in concern.

"The first time, you sounded so frightened, Bianca, I feared Fairfax had somehow found his way inside the house. You calmed as soon as I promised to keep you safe."

And kissed her too?

He gazed upon her with such tenderness that she couldn't quite muster the indignation she should, nor the bravado to accuse him of that offense as well. Even now, knowing Pierce had intruded while she slumbered, gratitude filled her more than anything else.

"I fear your secret might well be out, Pierce. Elsie knows about Miss Millie's mysterious appearances. Since she's checked my chamber a good number of times to locate the clever puss's secret entrance and found nothing, it won't take her long to figure out the obvious truth."

He'd not responded to her earlier remark about a

proposal yet.

Had he changed his mind already?

A brazen impulse gripped her. "I suppose there's only one way to salvage my good name now, isn't there?"

Footsteps echoed in the passageway, and moments later, Digby appeared with the fish, putting the conversation to a premature end. Much to Bianca's consternation, Pierce didn't broach the subject again, and though the rest of the meal passed in amiable conversation, regret shrouded her.

Nearly an hour later, after he coaxed almost every detail about her life from her, Bianca took a last bite of her cranachan. "I ate every speck, and I do believe it's the best I've ever tasted."

"Mrs. Digby will be well-pleased. I agree. It was scrumptious." Pierce tossed his serviette aside and rose. "I hope to talk you into a stroll through the gardens."

Overly full and more of a mind to find her bed and weep into her pillow than to engage in exercise of any kind, Bianca glanced at the drape-covered windows. Nightfall had occurred some time ago. "But surely it's dark as the Earl of Hell's waistcoat out there."

That rapscallion half-grin she couldn't resist appeared.

"Yes, but I have another surprise for you."

Bianca had never much cared for surprises, and this evening had abounded with them. But then again, most of those she'd experienced prior to tonight had led to heartache of some sort. Except for Luna, of course.

Pierce angled his head toward the dining room entrance, and Digby signaled to someone outside, then left the room.

"I've asked Elsie to fetch your new shawl," Pierce said as he pulled Bianca's chair out. "I promise, if it's too cold, we won't stay outdoors very long."

How could she resist?

His eyes all but danced with his merry secret.

"All right, but I cannot imagine what there is to see in that blackness." Waving her hand, she indicated the stark tobacco-brown festooned windows.

Joy lit his face, and he extended his elbow. "You shall see. And I think you'll be pleased. I hope you will be."

Little boy vulnerability softened the planes of Pierce's angular features. He would never admit it, but he longed for approval and acceptance. For unconditional love.

He had hers, if only Bianca dared tell him.

In the entry, Elsie helped wrap the shawl around Bianca's shoulders, and the maid and Pierce exchanged conspiratorial glances.

So, Elsie was in on whatever his scheme was. That explained why she suggested the bath, nap, and fragrant tea, and then took her sweet time in dressing Bianca and styling her hair.

"We'll exit through my study since it opens onto the back terrace." Pierce took Bianca's elbow again, leading her down the passageway.

Boyish excitement etched his features, and her resolve slipped further.

This attentive, caring rogue captivated her heart, and she was defenseless against him.

Once in the study, he guided her to the closed draperies.

"Now, I need you to trust me, Bianca. Close your

eyes, and keep them closed until I tell you to open them."

She dutifully shut her eyelids.

What in the world could there be to see?

Except perhaps as Halverstone was in the northern country, the night sky was especially clear, and they might see a few constellations. Or rarely, the northern lights.

Yes, that must be it.

A draft brushed her face as the draperies whisked open. The door latch gave way with a soft *click*, and a stronger, much cooler breeze buffeted her. Bianca shivered, grateful for the wrap.

Good thing Pierce thought to ask for her shawl.

He snaked one arm around her waist and cupped her elbow with his other hand.

"Keep your eyes closed," Pierce murmured near her ear.

Forever, if he kept his arm about her.

She inhaled his intoxicating cologne and trembled again.

"Bianca, I'm going to lead you onto the verandah

now. Mind your first step over the threshold."

Laughing, she said, "It's a good thing I trust you."

She did trust him. Unreservedly. And more. Much more.

God above, she did adore him. Even loved his rakishness and his thumbing his nose at society. Only an utter fool would turn down his proposal, and a vice squeezed her heart until she almost gasped from the anguish.

Oh, to be able to take back those rash words. The horrible accusations. The wounds her termagant's tongue inflicted.

A moment later, she stepped onto the flagstones, her shoes echoing hollowly. "Can I open my eyes now?"

"Not just yet." Pierce spoke into her hair, his breath warming her scalp. Such a simple thing, yet so intimate. He steered her a few more paces, then clasped her shoulders and turned her just so. "Now you may open them, my love."

Could he truly love her?

Bianca slowly lifted her eyelids and gasped.

"Oh, Pierce. It's breathtaking."

He'd done this for her?

After her cruelty this morning?

Tears welled, but not from sadness. Joy caused the moisture.

The terrace, the gardens, and even the pond glowed with scores of candles.

He gently squeezed her shoulders. "Elsie said you wanted to see Vauxhall or Convent Gardens at night. My grounds are not as magnificent, to be sure, but this was the best I could do in a short time with so few staff. I vow you shall visit both with me someday."

Blinking back a torrent of tears, she muttered, "Elsie babbles too much."

Where Pierce had come by so many candles and lanterns Bianca couldn't guess. The help must've spent hours preparing this. Likely the entire time she and Pierce were in Northhollow.

Even after she refused his proposal, he'd conspired to please her.

"I'm truly, truly touched, Pierce." She put a knuckle to the corner of one eye. "Thank you."

An odd sound, between a caterwauling feline and

an unoiled carriage wheel wafted to them from somewhere on the greens or gardens.

"What in Hades—?" She stood onto her tiptoes, peering into the orderly beds. Then scanned the lawns until her gaze came to rest upon the gazebo's domed top. A light reflected from within the arches.

"That would be Digby. Before he and his wife became domestics, they led a colorful life in the theatre." A particularly spine-tingling screeching note rent the calm, and Pierce hugged her from behind, chuckling. The thick wall of his chest resounded with his amusement. "Now I understand why he left the profession."

"I'd say he hadn't practiced in a goodly while." The strings squawked again, and Bianca twittered into her closed hand. She couldn't remember the last time she'd giggled. Angling her head, she glanced up at Pierce. "Do you know, Mrs. Digby had me fairly shaking in my shoes lest I do anything remotely improper? I thought, perhaps, that she is a person of strong faith, given the cross she wears at her neck."

He rotated Bianca so that they faced each other.

The moon illuminated half of his face, but the rest of his features remained hidden in the night's shifting shadows. "There's truth to that. According to Mrs. Digby, she and her husband realized the error of their ways, turned their lives over to the Lord, and set their minds to leading respectable lives. They've been trying to reform me since I hired them. Which is one reason I haven't been here in nearly five years, much to their chagrin."

Could rakes be redeemed?

Truly reformed? Did it matter?

Pierce had already beguiled her despite Bianca's efforts not to succumb.

She must know.

"Would that be so bad, Pierce?"

He cupped one side of her face with his powerful hand, running his thumb across her cheekbone, and she was powerless to move, much less resist.

"If you'd asked me that a month ago, my love, I would've laughed and called you every kind of fool. But now…" He drew her near until his hard thighs pressed into hers through her gown, and only an inch separated their torsos. "With the right woman by my side, I suspect there might be something to all that respectability rot. I would have you be that woman, Bianca."

This time, it was she who rose up on her toes and brushed his mouth with hers.

I've lost our bet.

~*~

Pierce had won.

The victory brought him no joy, but Bianca's sweetly offered kisses did.

He hesitated for a fraction of an instant before groaning and capturing her willing lips. Whereas their first kiss was tender and tentative, this meshing of mouths was a wild mating, hungry and sensual.

Bianca twined her arms around his neck and sagged into him.

Plunging his hand into her hair, he pulled the pins loose until the auburn cloud tumbled onto her shoulders and back.

The kiss went on and on, drawing him into a new dimension of yearning.

He'd suspected passion slumbered within her but hadn't expected this inferno of desire. She met each thrust of his tongue with her own, awkward at first but quickly acquiring the skill and learning the rhythm.

Did love make the pleasure so much more sensuous? Intense? Overwhelming and consuming?

Oh God, he did love the minx.

She whimpered and squirmed against him, her breath coming in hungry little pants.

Pierce clasped Bianca's shoulders and pulled his mouth away. Resting his forehead against hers, he rasped, "I must stop. I promised myself I'd be the perfect gentleman with you. You're too apt a pupil, my sweet, and I forget myself." Trembling, he pulled in a shuddering breath and whispered, "I would not have you loathe me for seducing you."

"I don't want you to be a gentleman. I know what this means. Elmswood is lost to me, but I don't care if it means I can stay with you." Eyes shining, Bianca caressed his cheek. "I don't want to leave you. Will you let me stay?"

Hope bloomed anew. Could she have changed her mind since this morning?

Was it possible?

For Pierce swore, she bore the expression of a woman in love.

A woman in love with him.

His soul soared to think such a thing was possible. That this unique, precious, and unpredictable woman might adore him as much as he cherished her.

With his forefinger, he touched her cheek, afraid to say the words again. He would know though. "Then you will marry me?"

A radiant smile blossomed across her face. "Tonight, if you wish."

Hugging her to him, Pierce laughed and lifted Bianca in the air, twirling her around and around. "Dear heart, I'm overjoyed. I meant to keep wooing you, to convince you that I love you."

Her hands braced upon his shoulders, she peered down at him, her smile gentle yet fragile. "I can hardly grasp that you really love me."

He let her slide to the ground as he whispered in her ear. "I do. I do. I don't know when you inveigled your way into my heart. It might've been that first night when you pleaded with me across the room to help you."

"You understood that?" Awe colored her voice and widened her eyes.

Pierce nestled her into the crook of his arm and clasped one of her hands within his. "I did. And so I did the only thing I could think of to make sure you were safe."

She tilted her head and gazed up at him.

"I wanted to hate you, but I couldn't. Somehow, especially after we arrived here at Halverstone, and you treated me so wonderfully, I knew the things I'd heard about you weren't true. Even this morning, when I spoke those hateful words to you, I didn't really believe them. I was afraid. Afraid to love you. That I'd end up a broken woman like my mother."

"I know, my sweet, and I know about your mother, too. Know the secret you've kept hidden for so long."

"You know she…?" Bianca swallowed audibly but forged on, the brave darling. "She sold her body?"

He nodded, his chin brushing the top of her head. "I vow I'll never leave you. Until the last breath leaves my body, I shall stay by your side."

Now wasn't the time to share the rest of the ugly tale about her parents, not when their love was so tender and new. Not when all Pierce wanted to do was worship Bianca, tell her all the things that had played through his mind in recent weeks.

She did need to know about Fairfax though, and so he told her.

"Honestly, Pierce, I find it sad and pathetic. He was toxic, spreading misery wherever he went. He couldn't have been happy, and his life seems such a waste." She sighed and cuddled closer, staring at the flickering candles, now burning low. "He was the last in his line, you know. The barony died with him."

"But don't you inherit everything as last of kin? If you wish, we can petition the king and ask him to appoint you the title." He searched her glowing face.

Bianca shook her head, the sultry cloud swishing about her shoulders.

"No, I'm perfectly content to be your wife." She cut

him a saucy glance. "Besides, a countess outranks a baroness."

"You'll also be a duchess one day."

That startled her, and she jerked her gaze to meet his. "Oh dear, I'm not sure I can do duchess. Countess pushed the mark for this country bumpkin."

"With me at your side, we can do anything together, my darling."

"What happens with the guardianship now?" she asked, a slight shadow darkening her features? "Can we marry if I don't have an official guardian to grant permission?"

He hugged her tight. "Well, it just so happens, I've been appointed your temporary guardian."

She chuckled against his chest, a musical burble of laughter.

He glanced downward, curving his mouth at the humor cavorting in her eyes. "Pray tell, what do you find so amusing?"

"I'm envisioning your sisters' reactions." She fingered his lapel and shook her head. "We cannot elope, you know. They would be devastated."

Pierce laughed then, too, and wrapped Bianca in his embrace once more. "My sisters would never forgive me if I denied them a wedding. Should we return to London on the morrow and make the announcement?"

"I think we must." She looked to the right and then to the left before grabbing his hand and pulling him toward the house.

"But first, I want a sample of the *much more* you mentioned in the carriage."

Epilogue

5 September 1817

Viscount and Viscountess Timberlys'

London

Pierce cradled Bianca's elbow as he and his glowing wife of two hours wended their way through the well-wishers crowded into Lenora's entrance and spilling out onto the stoop. The trio, their husbands, and a passel of noisy offspring chatted and beamed on one side, the wicked earls, Sutcliffe, Coventry and his countess, and their graces, the Duke and Duchess of Dandridge, the other.

The women and children smothered Bianca in hugs

and kisses as the men shook Pierce's hand, patted his shoulders, and congratulated him.

"I shan't say I told you so." Coventry winked, then cast an appraising glance at the other unshackled club members. "Who's next, do you suppose?"

Pierce chuckled and rubbed the side of his nose. "I'm sure you know that better than I and have already put your scheme into motion."

Lenora touched his forearm, then offered him a watery smile and a peck upon his cheek. "I knew from the instant I set my eyes upon your Bianca that she was a perfect match for you, Percy."

Rebecca embraced him next.

"I think she'll keep you well in hand, brother dearest. Be happy, Pierce," she whispered in his ear.

"How can I not?" he whispered in hers.

He turned to Amanda, her pregnancy evident now. He winked and gathered her near. "I think you should name this one after me, Mandy."

She shoved his shoulder playfully. "I cannot in good conscience name my daughter Rogue or Scoundrel."

Amidst a flurry of last-minute advice, tearful good-byes, and one or two slightly improper innuendos, Pierce swept Bianca into his arms.

Releasing a low laugh at her startled squeal, he carried her down the stairs, even daring a reverent kiss upon her peach-tinted lips. He signaled to Burroughs, then deposited her in the coach for their short journey to the London Docks. There, they would board a passenger ship bound for India for their wedding trip.

Once inside the carriage, Bianca untied her bonnet and removed her gloves and settled beside him. "I love you, Pierce."

He draped an arm around her shoulders and kissed the crown of her head. "I adore you too, my sweet. Best wager I ever placed."

"What would you have done if you hadn't won the game, Pierce?" she asked, tucking a stray curl behind her ear.

Shrugging, he stretched out his legs. "Abducted you, I suppose."

Though well before noon, the day promised to be warm. He cracked the windows, allowing fresh air into the stuffy conveyance.

"I finally read the rest of Uncle Sylvester's diary last night," Bianca said.

"He knew Mama had been forced to resort to prostitution, and he's the one who sent us money. Aunt Florencia never knew that he did." Bianca brushed her fingers up and down Pierce's muscled thigh. "She never forgave Mum for eloping with Papa and hated him for taking Mum from her. I suppose that's why Mum refused to return to Elmswood."

"I pity the lot." Pierce tilted her face upward, searching her umber eyes. A hint of sadness lingered there. "How are you faring? I know you didn't want to read your uncle's journal at first, but you needed to know the truth."

"Honestly, Pierce, I'm absolutely livid with them. Is that wrong?"

He made a soft sound of comfort. "No. They wronged you. Greatly."

"They're dead and buried, yet I've berated them in my head over and over for the suffering they caused Mum and me. My poor mum prostituted herself. They caused that and her death when they could've prevented both." She sighed, then in a small voice said, "It will be a long while before I am able to forgive them."

"Give yourself time to come to terms with their perfidy, darling." Pierce nuzzled her ear, gratified when she gave a little gasp. "I speak from experience. Harboring hatred and refusing to forgive only leads to bitterness."

"That's so true." She nestled closer, wrapping an arm around his waist. "I was surprised to discover that Salisbury is actually the viscountcy title and not my father's surname, Buchanan. He wasn't the heir, so I don't know why Papa chose to use that name. I'll never know, I suppose."

"Does that bother you?"

"No, not really." Bianca gazed out the window as the coach rumbled toward the wharf. Ship's masts lined the horizon. "I decided that today was going to be wonderfully happy, so nothing more I discovered could be that awful. I'm most appalled that Aunt and Uncle didn't tell Mum that Papa had been thrown from his horse after he secretly went to see them. I don't know if

Uncle felt guilty or if maybe, he suspected Aunt Florencia had something to do with the accident. She always did act peculiar whenever Papa was mentioned."

"At least you know for certain what happened to your father." Pierce grazed his thumb across the back of her hand.

"It does change how I feel about my aunt and uncle, though," Bianca murmured. "And I don't ever want to set foot at Elmswood Parke again."

He gave her shoulder a small squeeze. "I'll sell the place then."

"Pierce?" She bit her lower lip.

What made her so uncertain?

"What, my love? You can ask me anything." He grinned and tweaked her nose. "You know I can deny you nothing, sweeting."

"Can we donate the proceeds to helping women like my mother?" Sorrow thickened Bianca's voice. "Perhaps establish a home of some sort for them? If you hadn't rescued me, I might've become one of those unfortunate women."

He rubbed her spine with long, soothing strokes.

"Consider it done. I think it's a brilliant plan, truth to tell. I only held on to Elmswood for you."

The smile she bestowed upon him took his breath away.

It also magnified his guilt. He should've told her at Halverstone the night he surprised her with the lit garden and grounds. Afraid he might lose her, he'd kept mute.

"Bianca, I have a confession."

"Oh?" She leaned forward and peered at the ships as the vehicle rattled toward *The Night Swan's* berth.

"I kissed you the first night I sneaked into your bedchamber." He touched her cheek, an apologetic brush of his fingertips. "So you see, my sweet, you truly won our wager."

"I suspected as much." Bianca angled her head and grasped his hand. Giving him a naughty smile, she gently squeezed his fingers. "But I wanted you to teach me that *much more* bit."

Want a FREE first in series Starter Library
from Collette?

Go to: signup.collettecameron.com/TheRegencyRoseGift
to get a five FREE book bundle.

EARL OF SCARBOROUGH
For the Love of an Earl, Book Two

'Tis the season to be wicked…

When a woman desperate for a job saves the life of an earl…

… both of their plans for the future are thwarted.

He's eccentric and society-shy…

There's no polite way to describe Ansley, Earl of Scarborough's obsession with schedules and inflexible routines. Unfortunately, he's also in need of a wife, which forces him squarely in the midst of the society he can scarcely function within. If only he dared to ignore the *haut ton's* censure and claim the lovely, wholly unsuitable Willow as his own.

She seeks a governess post…

Up from the country, Willow Harwood must quickly secure a governess position and save enough money to return to America. Only, her plans are foiled when she rushes to the rescue of a devastatingly handsome earl in the process of being robbed. Though he's far above her station, she can't fight the irrepressible attraction she feels toward him.

Neither is prepared for the upheaval to their lives when she reluctantly accepts his offer of employment…as his housekeeper. Nor can either predict the mayhem that follows when a lord who disdains society and a country miss with no experience plan a *haut ton* Christmastide gathering.

Enjoy the first chapter of

EARL OF SCARBOROUGH

For the Love of an Earl, Book Two

October 1817

Wicked Earls' Club, London England

*B*ored. Bored. Bored.

Ansley Twistleton, the Earl of Scarborough, was bored. Out of his mind with *ennui*. Furthermore, he had absolutely no bloody idea whatsoever about how to remedy the situation. This discontentment. This restlessness. This new, entirely irksome, wholly vexing dissatisfaction. It made him edgy and irritable.

As was his habit, he analyzed his feelings logically and dispassionately. To a degree, he'd brought this state of malaise on himself. A man of rigid schedules and habits, nothing unexpected or exciting ever happened to him. That was precisely how he preferred his well-ordered, predictable life.

Until now.

Drumming his fingertips atop his thigh, he clamped his back teeth together, pondering the exasperating irregularity.

Why now? Why, after years of consistency, was he bored?

Probably, because his pursuits and interests were few.

He neither gambled nor frequented bordellos—*God only knew how many men those creatures of the boudoir had serviced*—nor did he racehorses. Assemblies, routs, balls, and the like were avoided like the plague or clap, as were picnics, the opera, musicals, and the theater.

Although... He'd been known to attend the latter by himself if the play consisted of something worth watching, and he made his way into his box before anyone had a chance to corner him into conversation. There was the inconvenience of having to wait until most of the other patrons had departed before he could make his escape. But on rare occasions, the performance had been entertaining enough to warrant the minor irritation.

To say he was socially awkward was as much an understatement as suggesting Caroline of Brunswick was out of favor with the portly Prince Regent, or the English had a slight partiality for tea.

Ansley's physical fitness and athleticism could be contributed to hours spent riding, fencing, and biweekly bouts of training at No.13 Bond Street with Jackson himself. Generally, those activities required little more than an occasional one-syllable-word comment, a grunt, or a noncommittal noise in the back of his throat.

Men never felt the need to blather on just to hear their own voices. And of colossal more importance, no primping, simpering, *salivating* females were ever in attendance.

God help him, but like hounds on the fresh scent of

blood, eligible young misses, their terrifying marriage-minded mamas, and their pernicious plotting papas had the habit of popping up at the most inopportune moments.

Much like disease-infested rats, cockroaches, or fleas.

One knew the loathsome pests lurked about in dark corners and crevices, but when one accidentally came upon one, the experience proved most alarming and unpleasant. Unlike *those* vermin which usually ended up dead, the giggling debutantes—God's bones how he detested giggling—were almost certain to appear again.

And again. *And again.* God help him and any other unattached male possessing a title.

Fingering his glass with its remaining dram of superior cognac, he rested his head against the wingback chair's plush crimson velvet. Legs crossed at the ankles, he stretched them before him and stared at the robust fire through half-closed eyelids.

Around him, the soft din of his fellow Wicked Earls' Club members' gaming, laughter, and conversations barely permeated his aura of jaded disinterest.

A wry smile kicked his lips up on one side. *Wicked earls, indeed.* His claims to wickedness were his cutting, sardonic tongue and wit. However, he couldn't vouch for the other earls one way or the other. He didn't know any of them well enough to form an opinion.

The trouble was, he decided, returning to the issue of his boredom with a slight downward slant of his mouth and a drink of the amber liquid, he eschewed most social gatherings. Consequently, he often found himself with nothing at all to do.

Until recently, that truth hadn't bothered him. He'd even declined to seek memberships at White's, Brooks, and Boodle's. As select as those gentlemen clubs were, they still allowed far too many members for his comfort.

Other than the secret Wicked Earls' Club and *Bon Chance*—another exclusive club and the only two places other than his country estate where he felt a degree of ease around other people—he avoided *le beau monde*.

Well, he didn't *willingly* entertain and mingle with the *haut ton*.

Since coming into his title seven years ago at the tender age of one and twenty, due to the premature death of his uncle, he'd been obligated to venture out on occasion. Very rare occasions. Mostly when his mother or sister entreated him to put on a mien of civilization. And loving them as much as he did, he tried to oblige their wishes every now and again.

He suspected they were the only two people entirely aware of what an immense effort it took each time to don his public persona. For he couldn't bear changes in his routines. Most particularly, unforeseen variations.

It rattled him in a way that was not only difficult to explain, but disconcerting and humiliating. Everything in his ordered life had a time. When he rose. Bathed. When he ate. What time he retired. When his hair was trimmed—every third Wednesday at half-past two. When he arrived at his clubs and, unsurprisingly, when he departed.

More than once, he'd wondered if he was even sane.

Surely such compulsions bordered on madness. A

terrifying notion that had haunted him since his youth.

At least he wasn't as dotty as that fellow who put on and removed his shoes five times before he'd leave his home and then checked to make sure the door was soundly locked by pushing the handle then the door itself in rapid succession four times.

No one—*bloody no one*—kept to habits as he did. Several times, he'd tried to ease his inflexibility and found himself a wreck. Tense. His nerves on edge. Unable to concentrate or relax. His oddity was a damn curse. Indeed, it was.

Oh, he could do it—if push came to shove. In fact, typically, no one was the wiser except those closest to him. But he preferred not to stray from routine if at all possible.

He dragged his eyes open and squinted at the white marble and gilt bronze clock. Exhaling a long breath, he levered himself upright in the chair and tossed back the remaining spirits. Time to leave. He set the glass aside, then shoved to his feet.

No one paid him much mind, which didn't bother him in the least. He enjoyed solitude. Craved it, in fact.

He'd wanted to be a scholar before inheriting the earldom—had hoped to teach Natural History and Ecclesiastical History at Oxford or Cambridge.

But earls didn't don austere robes and become professors. A rather irritating voice also dared remind him he mightn't have been able to stand before a hall of students and orate.

God's teeth. His own education had been as painful as hell, and he couldn't deny the truth. Despite his desire to teach, he lacked the wherewithal. No, that wasn't precisely correct. He possessed the knowledge but was without the ability to adequately communicate with or instruct a room full of pupils.

Reclining against the back of his usual chair beside the window, the Earl of Alcott smoked a cigar and stared morosely into his whisky tumbler. Somber, sad even, he raised the hand with the cigar toward Ansley in a silent farewell.

He acknowledged the salute with an elevated chin. Alcott was a decent chap. In fact, it was he who suggested Ansley join the Wicked Earls' Club.

Nonetheless, he hadn't ventured to the club tonight

for titillating conversation. Or any other night, for that matter. Not a bit of it. No, he forced himself out of his rather ostentatious Grosvenor Square house four nights a week, else he'd easily become a hermit, locked inside his comfortable home, playing the pianoforte, wasting time on billiards, and reading musty old tomes till time for bed.

Sounded like bloody bliss.

Another sardonic twist of his mouth followed his retrospection.

He rather liked the thought, truth be told. Why, he wouldn't even be required to shave or even dress, for that matter. All his meals might be taken in his banyan.

Recalling the correspondence from his mother this morning, *suggesting* the names of several eligible young misses that would make *"exceptionally, wonderful countesses,"* the tic near his left eye began twitching in earnest. A sure indication he was more upset than his outward façade of bored-nonchalance proclaimed. One would think he'd have become accustomed to the spasms, yet deep-rooted humiliation tumbled about in his stomach.

Dearest Mama had also recommended he host a Christmastide house party this year at Fawtonbrooke Hall, his country estate. He barely suppressed a shudder of distaste.

Horror of absolutely absurd horrors.

Guests tramping all about his sanctuary from dawn to midnight or later? Required to dine with them? Entertain the throng? Converse. *Dance*?

Absolutely not.

Bright-eyed misses with their coy smiles and simpering manners.

Hell on earth. A fate worse than death for a man like himself.

The muscle by his eye convulsed harder, and he angled his head toward the fireplace to hide the tremor lest it draw unsolicited attention. Disgust and anger at himself that he could yet be self-conscious of his— *inconvenience*—jabbed his pride.

Mama simply could not accept that at eight and twenty—nine and twenty in January—he possessed as much desire to wed as he did to have all of his teeth pulled. *Or be keelhauled. Tarred and feathered.*

Eviscerated with a hairpin. Burned at the stake. Hung by his ballocks.

A wife dragging him hither and yon, chattering like a magpie about nonsensical drivel, would drive him stark-raving mad. And what kind of a spouse would he be? Other than his title and passably good looks, he held no false illusions about his appeal or qualifications as a husband.

Or lack thereof.

In short, Ansley Cecil Huxley Twistleton, sixth Earl of Scarborough, was a stuffy, dour chap who broke into a cold sweat when in a room with more than a dozen or so people. A man who had as much skill with small talk as he did needlepoint or midwifery. A lord who'd been thrust into a life he had no more aptitude for than a hippopotamus did for ballet, or a cat for archery.

He was an oddity.

And, blast and damn, he shouldn't care.

About the Author

USA Today Bestselling author COLLETTE CAMERON® is renowned for her Scottish and Regency historical romance novels featuring daring rogues, scoundrels, and the strong heroines who capture their hearts. Her stories are filled with inspiration and humor, making them the perfect escape for fans of Sweet-to-Spicy Timeless Romances®. Living in Oregon, Collette is a confessed Cadbury chocoholic and dreams of spending part of her time in Scotland. From the rugged highlands to the refined drawing rooms of Regency England, Collette's stories transport you to another time and place, where love and adventure are just a page away.

Dearest Reader,

I'm so grateful you chose to read EARL OF WAINTHORPE. The inspiration for the story actually came from another book of mine, THE EARL AND THE SPINSTER, *The Misses Culpepper* series. That's another story about an ill-placed wager.

Pierce and Bianca are new characters to my readers, but the story does mention the Duke of Dandridge and the Duke of Sutcliffe, both of whom has their own books in my *Seductive Scoundrels* series.

Read the other *For the Love of an Earl* books:
EARL OF SCARBOROUGH
EARL OF KEYWORTH
EARL OF RENSHAW

To stay abreast of my other books' releases, subscribe to my newsletter, *The Regency Rose* (the link is below), or visit my author world at collettecameron.com.

If you liked Bianca and Pierce's story, please consider leaving a review. Reviews really do help authors.

Happy reading!

Hugs,